In an obscure Arab sta⸱ ⸱⸱gh Atlas,
Hasman Abdul⸱ah / ⸱ditary and
despotic ruler, h⸱ ⸱gotiated with
the Kremlin to ⸱ ⸱untry's natural
resources. Ri⸱ ⸱⸱, born of an
English mothe⸱ ⸱ed in England, is
Hasman's co⸱ ⸱rongly opposes his
plans. Alarn⸱ ⸱situation he has
created, Has⸱ ⸱⸱ony Dimarco and
his mob of ⸱ ⸱⸱rcen⸱ ⸱s, and a reign
of terror foll⸱ ⸱⸱asman ⸱ Dimarco the
task of liquid⸱ ⸱g Richar⸱ ⸱n but Tony,
adept at the d⸱uble cross, ⸱s to make
a private de⸱ ⸱ith Rich⸱

THE
MARKSMAN

by

Michael Cronin

Dales Large Print Books
Long Preston, North Yorkshire,
BD23 4ND, England.

British Library Cataloguing in Publication Data.

Cronin, Michael
    The marksman.

A catalogue record of this book is
available from the British Library.

ISBN   978-1-84262-736-5 pbk

First published in Great Britain in 1974 by
Robert Hale & Company

Copyright © Michael Cronin 1974

Cover illustration © Len Bernstein by arrangement with
Arcangel Images

The moral right of the author has been asserted

Published in Large Print 2009 by arrangement with
Michael Cronin, care of Watson, Little Ltd.

Dales Large Print is an imprint of Library Magna Books Ltd.

Printed and bound in Great Britain by
T.J. (International) Ltd., Cornwall, PL28 8RW

ONE

When the war ended Antonio Dimarco had been just another starving, skinny brat in the slums of Naples, born to thieve his way through life, to live on his wits and native cunning, like a rat in a crowded sewer.

He had done all of that, and more, and he still bore the marks of the conflict, inside himself. He had grown up tough and ruthless, making his own rules and to hell with anybody else.

He had many of the qualities that would make a good combat soldier, except for this matter of military discipline and taking orders, which did not square with his ideas of what was right and proper for Tony. He had tried it in his late teens – a short enlistment that had become even shorter because of the time he spent in the cells after breaking a corporal's jaw and insulting an officer who was unduly sensitive about the marital status of his parents, and Private Dimarco's discharge was rapid and with ignominy.

He had learnt nothing, except how to handle a gun efficiently and at speed – he had enjoyed that. He had the instincts of a bandit, all he needed was the right opening, and petty thieving was not the answer.

Eventually he moved north, to Milan and later Turin, where there was money being made. He got four years for attempted armed robbery of a super-market.

After that the best he could do for himself was as a pimp and occasional strong-arm boy in a sporting-house. It gave him no real scope for his talents. There had to be other things, and the world was wide, and the best part of it must be elsewhere.

He signed on as a deck-hand in Genoa on a ship bound for the Mexican Gulf. All the way over he had to watch himself because the crew were bastards and the mate the worst of the lot. He jumped ship at Vera Cruz, which had been his idea from the first, after rifling the pockets and wallets of most of his shipmates. He would need financing.

In due course he got himself smuggled across the border into the USA, the home of free enterprise where a smart boy could go places fast so long as he was quick on his feet. Dollars.

He made some early mistakes, but they were all part of his education in the way a racket should be run to the maximum of profit. He worked hard to get himself accepted by some of the big outfits as a coming boy with a lot of nerve.

He had the right background and he looked good – a big man with plenty of dark, curly hair and nice teeth. A stud with no papers. Hustling. Picking up a dollar here and there.

For a while he lived with a rich widow in a nice place in Bel Air and did no work outside the bedroom. That was okay for a while. The widow was fifty but she had looked after herself and she could still make it interesting enough. Tony picked up some better forms of English, and the widow got him to dress less obviously and in better taste. She picked up all the bills and made him a handsome allowance.

She even wanted to marry him, but her only son in Detroit came into the picture and raised vigorous objections, so Tony beat him up just a little right there in front of the lady.

At the sight of her only offspring lying there senseless and bleeding all over her pretty carpet, the widow had a change of

7

heart and began to make hostile noises. She reached for the phone in an unfriendly fashion.

'You've killed him,' she lamented. 'You brute! Look what you've done to him! Oh my God, this is terrible – I'll get the police and an ambulance–'

Tony hauled her away from the phone. 'Listen, baby,' he said, 'I did it on account of you and me, he was trying to bust us up, that mean nothing to you? Be your age, baby.'

That was the final insult, reminding her that she was over twenty years his senior. She kicked him sharply on the shin and she still swung a nifty shoe.

So Tony had to let her have one on the button to quieten her down. He dumped her on the bed where he had been earning his keep, collected all the loose cash he could find – nearly a thousand dollars, some of her jewels, and took off in her red Thunderbird.

Enough was enough. She'd been getting in his hair. All that fuss just because he had to spread momma's boy around the floor. Silly old cow.

He parked the Thunderbird down in the town and walked to the bus depot. He bought himself a through ticket on the Greyhound going east. Chicago would be okay for him. She wouldn't do anything about whistling in the pigs because then it would all have to come out and that would do her reputation no good. That had been sonny boy's big objection – what would people think if she married a man half her age? Trash like Tony Dimarco, obviously a hoodlum, and so on.

They would write it off to experience and maybe she would be more careful in the future.

Tony was asleep in his seat when the bus made a stop up-country and the troopers came aboard, two of them with holsters unbuttoned. They collected Tony and took him back.

The widow proved herself no lady and told all in court, so that Tony appeared the lousiest of bastards who seduced a lonely widow, grievously assaulted her only son when he tried to protect his mother's fair name, and then robbed the unfortunate lady into the bargain.

He was also illegally in the country, which made him highly undesirable on every count. He did his time in San Quentin, and was then escorted out of the country.

Africa beckoned. There was room there and action and no nonsense about your past record. In the Congo he carried a gun along with other white mercenaries, and did more than his share of shooting and looting, and the lack of discipline suited him fine.

He began to acquire a reputation, and there was always some scene where he could find employment in an irregular capacity. If the money was right there was very little that Tony Dimarco would not undertake, and he began to attach to himself a little band of tough operators who followed him because he had the look of a winner, and he had the knack of making the right kind of bargain with those who held the money bags for the time being.

Like an astute politician, dealing with the sharp realities of life and sudden death, Dimarco had developed a nose for the party likely to come out on top, and thus never hesitated to switch sides when the time was ripe.

Biafra was okay for a while, but it folded too soon and outside folk started sticking their noses in and bringing in television cameras where they had no business to be.

By this time Tony Dimarco was a character

in his own right, big and heavily bearded like a real jungle fighter, and worth cultivating if you had an awkward thing in your way, like somebody you would rather do without. Tony would take care of it, for a price, and he didn't come cheap. But you knew there would be no unpleasant repercussions. No bodies turning up dead in the wrong place. They would remain sadly mourned and not accounted for. Which is no more difficult to arrange in Africa than anywhere else when you know your business.

Relaxing in Takoradi, with the nucleus of his retinue, Tony made his mark with a variety of women, particularly the ones who considered themselves sophisticated. He was barbaric and so virile, and if he fancied the lady his approach was unsubtle and direct: yes or no, lady – don't mess me about, even if her husband was present. And he met with a high percentage of acceptances. The combination of his appearance and the climate was devastating to frail virtue, and few husbands had the nerve to resist his invasion of their preserves. There was always that little mob in the background, and the suburbs of Takoradi were not well lit or patrolled.

Smuggling, gun-running, and associated

lawlessness, had Dimarco and his group working their way north wherever there was a disturbance that could be turned to profitable use. Soldiers of fortune in their own truck. Saluting no flag. Cash in advance.

Tony Dimarco's career was colourful and full of incident, but it was lacking in direction until he met Hasman Abdullah Ahmin, in Casablanca.

Hasman Ahmin was an aristocratic Arab, hereditary ruler of a small Sultanate named Ahminad after the family that had run its fortunes for some generations. It was a small feudal enclave round which the wind of change had been blowing up through the foothills of the Middle Atlas, from the continent beyond.

As his forefathers had done before him, Hasman Ahmin had been resisting change, and he intended to continue as the absolute ruler.

However, in recent years mineral deposits had been located in useful quantities – copper of a high grade, bauxite, and, of course, oil. Also there was an excellent deep-water anchorage that could easily become one of the best harbours on that stretch of the coast.

Ahminad was going to go commercial, and Hasman Ahmin was finding himself the target of powerful outside pressures, all anxious to push the Sultanate into prosperity.

Hasman himself favoured the Russians. They were offering the best deal, he thought: development loans, long-term credit, teams of technical experts, and all with no political strings attached, so Hasman had been assured.

Other interests – from the USA and Britian and France – were less than happy at the thought of the Kremlin having another toe-hold in that area. There was the uneasy picture of Russian warships and aircraft carriers and submarines sitting in wait, ready to slam the door on the Mediterranean if and when the time came.

So the inevitable tug-of-war had been taking place, with Hasman Ahmin in the middle holding the hankie; far more important than he had ever expected to be.

The Ahminad interest was not confined to Hasman himself. There was an opposition, very vocal and increasing in numbers among the younger inhabitants. They had crazy ideas about votes and free speech and the emancipation of the workers, dangerous democratic nonsense. They wanted free schools and hospitals and a medical service for the poor. They actually wanted some say in what was happening to their little country, and they were becoming very militant in their opposition to Hasman Ahmin's negotiations with the Russians because they said that once the Russians got in they would never get out.

They found their leader in Richard Ahmin, a cousin to Hasman, the son of an English mother and educated in England. Richard was ten years younger, and he had recently come back to Ahminad, where he had soon won a popular following. He was pro-British and strongly anti-Russian, and he had been making his presence felt.

Ahminad had never had a parliament, just a Council of State composed of landlords, mostly elderly conservatives who did as the Sultan ordered.

There was a small army which doubled as a police force, and of which Hasmin Abdullah Ahmin was hereditary Commander-in-Chief. It was poorly paid and badly equipped, and the junior officers were of doubtful loyalty even after a series of purges.

The opposition had begun to do more than hold subversive meetings and make angry speeches. There had been attempts on Hasman Ahmin's life – shots had been fired at his car, and some of them had been too close for comfort. Arrests had been made, but even Hasman himself knew they had never got the men responsible.

The Council State were getting jittery, and some of the more senile members had retired to their estates for safety. And Hasman had found it prudent to restrict his public appearances.

There was an occasion when the State limousine had been blown up a few minutes before Hasman was due to ride in it, right there in front of his official residence. The Chief of Police and the chauffeur had been the only occupants, and there had been nothing much left to bury. Not that the Chief of Police had been any great loss.

Ahminad was tottering into a state of civil war, and the Russian trade delegates were pressing Hasman to do something about it if he hoped to see the colour of their money. They did not propose to invest their roubles in a state that was about to collapse.

The rumour was becoming widespread – there would be no peace in Ahminad until

15

Richard Ahmin sat in the seat of power. He was the man. Hasman Abdullah Ahmin's era had passed. He was still living in a bygone century.

The Russian delegates were unable to understand why Hasman didn't adopt the obvious course – remove Richard, liquidate him.

Hasman compromised. He was reluctant to make Richard into a martyr, so he ordered him into strict house arrest, to be held incommunicado, under an armed guard. This enabled Hasman to pose as a merciful ruler. Later, a more permanent solution would be found. And the Russian negotiators would be happy.

Hasman's immediate problem now was to tighten up his own domestic security, since he did not look forward to offering himself as a target to any disgruntled agitator with a gun – the time might well come when one of them wouldn't miss.

He needed professional assistance, and he knew he could only get it from outside Ahminad. He had to have somebody with no local ties, an independent operator who would owe loyalty only to Hasman Abdullah Ahmin.

Somebody tough and experienced, who would not mind getting his hands dirty.

He remembered the man he had met in Casablanca a month before. Antonio Dimarco.

He didn't send for him, because the postal service was unreliable and the telephone even worse. He drove privately down to Casablanca, and he caught Tony at a good moment with no engagement on hand and with overheads still to be met.

He put the proposition to him. He was to be Hasman's own personal appointment. Bodyguard and Chief of Secret Police with the rank of Colonel, and at a rate of pay three times what any Police Chief had ever enjoyed before in Ahminad. Plus fringe benefits and privileges that made the offer attractive indeed.

Tony looked the proposition over and liked it. He would be going legitimate for the first time in his life, and for a handsome return. The notion amused him. Colonel Tony Dimarco. Licensed to knock off anybody and they couldn't put a finger on him.

They had met in Hasman's suite in the best hotel on the sea front, and Hasman, who didn't drink himself, had been lavish in his hospitality. Furthermore, he had put on the table by Tony's chair a neat little block of clean notes, five thousand dollars, which he referred to as a signing-on fee for Tony's exclusive use.

'Okay,' said Tony. 'You got yourself a deal, boss. I got some good boys I want to bring in with me – they'll have to be made into officers, lootenents and suchlike – that okay with you?'

Hasman nodded. 'I have confidence in your judgement, Colonel. You will need reliable assistants.'

Tony grinned at this instant promotion. 'I handle all of it in my own way?'

Hasman nodded.

'No outsiders squealing? There's gonna be some red faces when we move in?'

'You will report only to me,' said Hasman. 'Direct. Nobody in Ahminad will dare to interfere.'

'I like that,' said Tony.

'My personal safety will be your first duty. Ahminad has been in a state of unrest, I look to you to cure it, and you will take what measures you see fit. I will have no more disturbances.'

'That makes sense,' said Tony. 'We'll chop them down to size. You scared, boss?'

He was genuinely interested in this slight,

dark featured man with a long, impassive face and the dark, watchful eyes. A proper high-class Arab. You couldn't miss that. It might be difficult to fool a guy like him in his own territory. Most Arabs were tricky. You had to nail them down hard. That was Tony's experience.

'It does not suit my plans to die just yet, Colonel Dimarco,' said Hasman. 'That is why I am here to engage your services. I will expect to have first call on you at any time. There will be opposition and you will not be popular in my country – I have some violent people.'

Tony grinned widely. 'You bet. We don't play it soft, either.'

'This is a personal arrangement between you and me, Colonel, it concerns nobody else. I will be paying for service and I will expect service.'

'That's right,' said Tony. 'And if I got a beef I bring it straight to you, okay?'

'If anything happens to me,' said Hasman Abdullah Ahmin, 'there are people in my country who will gladly hang you and your men from the nearest tree, and they will mutilate you slowly first.'

'That figures,' said Tony. 'We wouldn't expect anything else. It has to be rough all

19

round and that suits us.'

Hasman's thin lips parted in a faint unpleasant smile. 'So you will see that nothing happens to me.'

Tony leaned forwards, scooped up the packet of notes, slapped them against his palm reflectively.

'I can round up the boys by tonight. When do we start? I got a truck and a good boy to drive. We'll clean up Ahminad real good.'

'I hope so,' said Hasman. 'Report to me at my Residence by sunset two days from now. I will arrange suitable accommodation. This is not to be talked about beforehand. Understood?'

'Check,' said Tony.

'You will leave it to me to advise those who should know about you. There will be no idle talking on your side.'

'Check again.'

'You will bring nobody you cannot fully trust.'

'Any guy I don't trust I dropped along the way,' said Tony. 'We been in business a long time, boss–'

'You will call me Excellency, always in public.'

'Anything you say. You're the boss, Excellency. You give us a square deal and everything will go okay. You put the finger on anybody giving you trouble and you got my word – we'll take care of him, permanent.'

'That is my intention,' said Hasman Abdullah Ahmin.

TWO

Within a week Tony Dimarco and his circus were established. They had a requisitioned property near His Excellency's Residence, with a separate apartment for the Colonel and a private line direct to the Residence. They had been issued with distinctive uniforms, a very splendid one for the Colonel with a Sam Browne.

There was speculation and criticism of these new arrivals, but those nearest to Hasman Ahmin had learnt to keep their mouths shut, at least in public.

There was no constitution, so what Hasman had done was not unconstitutional – it was an emergency security measure, and Hasman made it clear that Colonel Dimarco had his full support.

At their first appearance in the streets, Tony rode high on the back of a jeep, in full uniform, cradling a sub-machine gun, in front of the official car, inviting any mug to take a pot shot. Nobody did. And this became the pattern for Hasman's appearances.

The editor and proprietor of Ahminad's only newspaper was unwise enough to print some disparaging comments on their ruler's new bodyguard. So Tony drove down to the newspaper office in broad daylight and in uniform, he pinned the editor to his own desk and broke most of his teeth with his own ruler, then he sat on the desk while the boys worked through the office. It was just like the good old days, only this time they wouldn't have to beat it when they heard the siren.

Ahminad would have to get along without its press. And a little reign of terror was under way. To keep the boys on their toes Tony set up a series of searches of selected properties, allegedly for hidden arms, and the properties were always those of the citizens known to be hostile to Hasman's régime, so it was fruitless to protest. They never found any weapons, but they made plenty of enemies.

Inside two weeks Tony had his first casualty. One of his lieutenants, a young German named Bacher ignored the Colonel's instruction about not working alone at night. He was in bed with the wife of a sanitary engineer who was supposed to be up-country on a sewage job. The husband returned a night too soon, and shot Bacher with Bacher's own gun, then his wife, and then himself to make it a full score.

'Let that be a lesson to you guys,' said Tony to his men. 'Any time you want to get laid you do it here, in barracks, that's an order.'

At Tony's insistence, Hasman imposed a temporary curfew: the streets had to be cleared by ten o'clock at night. Colonel Dimarco alone was authorized to issue permits to be abroad, and the underground opposition slapped up posters denouncing this further infringement of the liberty of the citizens.

Then Tony developed the habit of dropping in uninvited on any social gathering he heard about, all in the line of duty, usually to the manifest embarrassment of host and hostess. He would swagger about in uniform, unsnubbable and impervious to icy stares and whispered comments, popping awkward questions at all and sundry. If there was a woman there who interested him he might invite her back to his apartment, for a night-cap, and so forth.

On one of these occasions he took an immediate fancy to a girl he had never seen before. A slim, blonde girl with dark blue eyes and a beautifully tanned skin. She was class right the way through. Partly French. Real chic. And when he heard her name his interest increased, because Louise Vannier was known to be Richard Ahmin's girl.

She was rich and well-educated, and a real snooty beauty. Right from the start she made it very clear she was not at all impressed by the Colonel's personality and that she found his bandit manners ludicrous.

She refused to dance with him – and that hurt because Tony happened to be a very good dancer. She wouldn't drink with him, and she ignored his conversation quite pointedly.

She wore a cream dress and already he was imagining how she would look without it on his bed. She had nerve all right, and style. He had never before met a beautiful woman who could look right through him like that as though he wasn't there.

When she walked away he couldn't look at anybody else in the room. She made them all look like rag dolls with powdered faces. Now there was one he just had to have, somehow. It wouldn't be easy. But it would be worth it.

She had recently come to Ahminad, and that was because of Richard Ahmin. She would certainly want to get in touch with him, perhaps she even hoped she would be allowed to see him. That was the kind of girl she was – plenty of spirit.

She was staying at the only respectable hotel in the place, and Tony detailed one of his young men to watch her and see where she went and what she did, and if that got on her nerves it would also show her she wasn't fooling around with a nobody, by God.

Tony had already paid an official visit to the house where Richard Ahmin was confined, and he thought very little of the security arrangements. So Hasman had allowed him to put one of his men in charge to inject a little ginger into the sloppy guards.

There was a high wall all round the house and a gate that was kept locked and guarded. Richard Ahmin was let out into the grounds each day for exercise, but now Tony's man went with him, and the grounds were being patrolled night and day.

When Richard Ahmin first met Tony Dimarco he was frankly amused and not at all inclined to take him seriously. And Tony knew instinctively that this lounging young man in the pretty pale blue shirt and the beige tapered slacks was no light-weight. He was too British, and Tony had had some dealings with the British. They had a knack of being tougher than they looked. And tricky.

They had been on top of the heap so long, and it wasn't all over for some of them. Like this one for instance. Half Arab, maybe. But mostly British.

'My dear chap,' said Richard Ahmin, 'do come in. What a perfectly splendid uniform. Where did you get all those ribbons? You must be the new functionary I have been hearing about. Colonel, isn't it?'

Tony knew it would be no use to act insulted, so he grinned. His medal ribbons would not bear inspection by anybody who knew about decorations, but a Colonel had to have something on his chest.

'They looking after you okay in here?' he said.

'Adequately,' said Richard.

'Nice place,' said Tony, looking round the tasteful room.

'It ought to be,' said Richard. 'It's my own property.'

'Plenty of people think you're too comfortable here. They'd sooner see you in jail.'

'No doubt,' said Richard smiling. 'I'd offer you a drink, but my supplies have been confiscated. Do you bring me a message from my loving cousin, Colonel? How is the dear Sultan? Still worried?'

'He's alive,' said Tony. 'And he's gonna stay that way.'

Richard Ahmin settled himself in an elegant lounging chair. He made Tony feel clumsy and uncouth, which normally didn't bother Tony because it didn't occur to him.

'Do please sit down,' said Richard. 'You intimidate me, standing there in that gorgeous outfit.'

'You got a hell of a nerve for a prisoner,' said Tony. 'How does a guy like you pass the time in here by yourself?'

'I read,' said Richard. 'I have music with my collection of records. My mother lived in this house at one time, so it has sentimental associations for me.' He smiled at Tony. 'So you are here to guarantee my cousin's immortality – I hope he is paying you well, Colonel. I fear it is likely to prove a short-term assignment.'

'I wouldn't put any money on you,' said Tony.

'A soldier of fortune, imported to preserve the tottering régime of Hasman Abdullah Ahmin, whom God will have to preserve because most of the people of Ahminad wouldn't lift a finger for him. Have a cigar, Colonel. You will find none better around here. As you will have discovered, Cousin Hasman neither smokes nor drinks, and women leave him cold.'

Tony selected a long, pale cigar from the humidor. It was better than he was used to.

'You're lucky to get tobacco,' he said. 'You don't get cigars like this in jail.'

'My own supply,' said Richard. 'I also pay for my own food and the servants are mine as well – a quaint local custom, it has its advantages. Are you happy in your work, Colonel?'

'You make with the funny jokes,' said Tony. 'It don't bother me – you're the guy out of circulation, not me.'

'You've been in the States,' said Richard pleasantly. 'I wonder how the Mafia manages without you.'

'I'm laughing,' said Tony.

'We must see more of each other,' said Richard. 'If I grovel at your feet do you think you could persuade dear Hasman to let me have back a bottle of Scotch? Or aren't you that important?'

'Like I said, you're not short on nerve.'

'Hope springs eternal.'

'You're sitting on a volcano,' said Tony. 'You could get yourself rubbed out, no trouble at all.'

Richard Ahmin nodded his complete agreement. 'I think of nothing else in the still watches of the night. Do you see yourself as the executioner, Colonel Dimarco?'

'I wouldn't lose any sleep, you got my word for that.'

'It's all in one's point of view – is that why you're here, to warn me of my impending dissolution?'

'I met a friend of yours the other day. Nice girl.'

Richard smiled gently and tapped the clean ash from his cigar.

'She could get herself deported,' said Tony thoughtfully. 'If she tries to get in touch with you we'd have to ease her out, know what I mean?'

'You have everybody searched before they come here,' said Richard. 'Even my food is inspected.'

'Don't give me that crap,' said Tony. 'You're getting information passed in to you.'

'You're a crude bastard, Colonel Dimarco.'

Tony grinned. 'And how would you like a poke in the puss?'

'I'm so glad we understand each other. I hear the climate outside has been a little stormy since you arrived. A word of warning to you, Colonel – you haven't met the real opposition yet.'

'You mean you?' said Tony. 'I'm still laughing. If Hasman did what I told him you could say your prayers.'

'I like your outlook, so direct and refreshingly simple.'

'I don't fool around and I get results,' said Tony.

'Another glimpse of the obvious. So Hasman has instructed you to get rid of me, is that it?'

'Would you be surprised?'

'Not in the least.' Richard Ahmin still retained the light and slightly amused tone.

'You get in his hair,' said Tony. 'He's got this big deal cooking, you spoil it, you and your mob–'

'–Patriots, please,' said Richard in a pained voice. 'We are the progressives, my dear man – we wish to see our country emerge from the middle ages, and without

31

Russian help.'

'You'll never swing it,' said Tony. 'Hell, a lotta sheep, that's what I think of you people here – you'll never amount to anything. Hasman cracks the whip and you all jump.'

'A word in your ear, Colonel,' said Richard. 'If ever you feel inclined to venture outside the town into the hills, make sure you have an armoured vehicle and reliable soldiers with you – some of our sheep have Berber blood in their veins, they have an awkward tradition of resisting outsiders, especially mercenaries. You would not care to die with your manhood stuffed in your mouth, crucified on some barren hillside: a regrettable custom and not at all Christian.'

'You talk real good,' said Tony. 'I never yet met the Arab who could make me back down … and you're only half a one yourself. Like me to take any message to your girl?'

'I doubt if she needs to be aware of your existence, Colonel, and if that sounds like an insult it is merely that I cannot tolerate the thought of you being in the same room as the lady in question. You do not inhabit the same world.'

Tony's grin widened. 'So what do you figure you can do about it, stuck in here? You're a dead duck. You shouldn't be talking so big.'

Leaning forward in his chair, Richard Ahmin said softly, 'if I hear anything that I don't like, Colonel Dimarco, the next time you come in here you should be ready to use that gun in your holster.'

'Check,' said Tony. 'A pleasure to do business with you. You reckon you can take over the outfit here? It's loaded against you.'

'Is it?' said Richard. 'You know nothing about this country and its people. Hasman hired you to protect his own skin. You've scared a few people, just a few, and they don't matter, they are the ones who will always be ready to run. You may stop people taking shots at Hasman for a while.'

'It's my business to keep him alive,' said Tony. 'You can wrap your goddam politics into a bundle and blow them through the key-hole, makes no difference to me – while Hasman meets my payroll he's okay with me.'

'You picked a loser, Colonel. Hasman is right out of touch with the world he lives in.'

'I must remember to tell him,' said Tony. 'But you don't look much like a winner – you could be heading for the big chop.'

Richard Ahmin stood up. He didn't look worried. He was tall, not heavily built, much lighter than Tony. Pale blue eyes and a straight nose. Nothing soft about his mouth. Tony decided that he looked more of a natural-born boss than his cousin. He might be half a foreigner, he acted like a playboy. But he wouldn't fold up easily.

'Well, Colonel,' he said, 'it's been terribly nice meeting you like this, I see so few visitors, and I have been wondering what kind of a man you were.'

'You reckon you know now?'

'You interest me, as a specimen of the soldier of fortune – efficient but without conscience: am I being too harsh?'

'Tough talk,' said Tony cheerfully. 'Were you thinking of making me an offer?'

Richard smiled. 'You don't disappoint me.'

'That's good,' said Tony, also standing.

'I admire your business instinct, Colonel – no frills. As straight as a bullet.'

Tony nodded at the tribute. 'Now wouldn't it be a hell of a thing if I got instructions from His Excellency to stick you behind bars – we only got one jail here and it's real lousy.'

'His Excellency?' said Richard. 'My, my, how very feudal. Ten thousand American dollars, credited to any bank you care to name – does that begin to interest you?'

'Maybe,' said Tony. 'You sure you can deliver?'

'On the word of half an English gentleman. I have seen the jail here, Colonel, strictly as a privileged visitor. It does not entice me.'

'I'll let the girl know you're okay, for the time being.'

Richard Ahmin's blue eyes were suddenly frosty.

'Stay away from her. I would prefer you to assure His Excellency my dear cousin that I am in good spirits.'

'Be a load off his mind,' said Tony. 'You could have it a hell of a sight worse.'

'I could,' said Richard, 'but I am not a criminal, Colonel. I am a political detainee.'

'Don't lean on it too hard.'

'Tell Hasman that I still do not intend to bring any shame on an honourable name, the name I share with him, unfortunately.'

'Sounds good,' said Tony.

'Remind him there are plenty of honest men in Ahminad who will see that our little country does not become just another appendage to the Russians, no matter what they are offering him. Can you remember that?'

Tony adjusted his gleaming Sam Browne. 'You're nuts.'

'Only on my mother's side.' Richard Ahmin's face was bland as his voice. 'She left me the money, Colonel. I am something of a capitalist, the kind of person you probably pretend to despise.'

'You making a speech?' said Tony.

'Do forgive me,' said Richard. 'You wouldn't be a dedicated Communist, by any mischance, would you?'

'Me?' said Tony, a little affronted. 'Man, you gotta be joking. Politics stink.'

'You may have a point,' said Richard.

'I operate strictly for Number One, Tony Dimarco.'

'Very sensible. So you have realized that as soon as Hasman feels reasonably secure you will be out of a job?'

'Do I look that dumb?'

'You will then bear in mind the matter we have been discussing?'

'I don't forget money talk,' said Tony.

'A man after my own heart.'

Tony looked at him hard. This guy used a lot of words, and he had that polite smile on his face, sort of superior. He might turn out to be a hell of a sight trickier than his cousin.

'Have we an understanding?' said Richard pleasantly.

'Don't rush me,' said Tony. 'There's some angles I have to work out.'

'We may not have too much time. Ahminad begins to bubble, Colonel. The Russians are still with us – have you met them yet?'

'I don't meddle with those bastards,' said Tony.

'You may not have the choice much longer. They are pushing Hasman.'

'You get good information in here,' said Tony.

'One must keep in touch,' said Richard mildly. 'After all, I am supposed to have influence, of a sort ... so I hear things.'

They walked over to the door, a polite host seeing his guest off the premises. The door leading into the hall was closed and they both knew there was an armed guard out there.

'I'll tell you this for free,' said Tony. 'The day those commie bastards move in here you get the chop.'

'So I imagine.'

'You're a luxury they don't want to afford.'

'Sad,' said Richard Ahmin. 'Will I see you again, Colonel?'

'Soon.' Tony opened the door into the hall and nodded at the young Lieutenant outside who raised his automatic in greeting and grinned.

'One of my own guys,' said Tony. 'Lootenant Prystocki from Posnan. Nice guy but kind of trigger-happy, if you know what I mean. He'd plug you soon as look at you. That right, Lootenant?'

'Sure thing.'

Lieutenant Prystocki strolled over and held out his hand. He had the build of an athlete and a strong abrupt handshake.

'I watch him good, Colonel,' he said, smiling as though promising the best of good fortune to Richard Ahmin.

'You better,' said Tony.

As he walked out into the sharp sunshine to his car, he was already considering how he could collect ten thousand dollars without risking anything else His Excellency Hasman Abdullah Ahmind might have in mind for him.

Play them both for suckers. Both ends against the middle. Why not? Now that would be real politics.

THREE

There was a party of three in the jeep, doing the road survey through the hills. Ahminad had almost nothing that could be called a road in modern terms. Just dirt tracks that had carried traffic for over two thousand years – the legionaries, camel caravans, adventurous merchants with their wares, sad lines of slaves chained together, pilgrims who had made it to Mecca or Jerusalem, refugees from the onslaught of the centuries hoping for freedom if only they could reach the sea down there beyond the harsh hills.

Soon the bulldozers and earth-movers and mechanical grabs and teams of explosive experts would be moving in, to blast their way through, to level and grade and establish a surface that would carry heavy, modern traffic down to the sea.

Two men and a girl, Galina, the girl, sat by the driver, Kurylin, a young man her own age. Borlov, the senior surveyor, in the late forties, dozed on the back seat with some of their gear, undisturbed by the bumping;

Borlov could sleep anywhere at any time when he was not actually working, which made him rather unexciting company.

All the three of them were in their working clothes, khaki shirts and shorts and high, lace-up boots. Galina was a plump blonde with chopped hair and a short nose, and heavy thighs that filled her shorts. When cleaned-up and dressed in suitable clothes, she could make a presentable appearance. She was also good at her job and expected no favours just because she was female.

Their truck had gone on ahead of them, and the jeep was making a detour because there was a section Borlov was not happy about, so they were going to take another look at it before they drove down to the town. They were all hot and tired and dirty.

When Kurylin pulled off the track where the grey rocks climbed up into the scrub, Galina got out and eased her shorts away from her hot thighs, and the back of her shirt was dark with sweat.

Borlov followed her quite briskly. He said he was going to climb further up and get a better view. There was an easier line than the one they had provisionally mapped out – he was sure of it because he had worked in hills like this before.

They let him start up, and he went faster than either of them would have done, his thin legs remarkably agile and sure.

Galina moved across and found some shade under an overhang of rock. The track wound around a line of hills, and Borlov was probably right – they needn't work so high, they could slice through the rock lower down, saving gradient and mileage.

Kurylin joined her under the rock, he was offering her a cigarette when in the clear air they heard the sharp crack of a rifle up above. Kurylin dropped his case and they both scrambled out.

Borlov's body was moving, slowly rolling down, like a half-filled sack. It gathered speed as it reached a smoother piece of rock. Then it lodged, head down, legs sliding sideways.

They could see nothing else, and the sun was throwing deceptive shadows among the broken rocks up there.

Kurylin whispered to Galina to stay where she was, he made one move to start climbing to where the body lay, because Borlov might still be alive and young Kurylin was no coward. There was another shot, to their left, and rock splintered in their faces.

So they dropped down to where they had

been. Kurylin held up two fingers warningly: the two shots had come from different directions.

They had a rifle in the jeep. They had strict instructions – whenever they drove out into the hills somebody had to be armed; with their working party in the truck there was a sub-machine gun.

So far the record had been easy. There had been a half-hearted attempt at an ambush a week before – a few random shots at a truck on a blind bend. No damage and no casualties.

The jeep was in full sunlight, some sixty feet away. They would have to reverse it on to the track, if they could reach it, and they would be in the open.

How many of them were there up there waiting? Much better shots than the other lot. Was it just a hit-and-run episode. Had they now cleared off?

Galina and Kurylin waited, it was all very quiet, not even birds to sing, no trees up there. The jeep waited for them, the sunlight glinting off its windscreen.

Galina checked the man-sized watch on her wrist. Ten minutes since it had begun. She had been shot at before, but always in bigger company – with men who had returned the fire with interest. This was different. Just the two of them, and a gun they were not likely to reach. Unless their ambushers had taken off over the other side.

They discussed the possibility. Bandits had little strategy, usually. They had met with a small success, that might be enough for them.

Kurylin nodded at the jeep. 'They would like to take that.'

Galina shoved the sweat-darkened hair away from her forehead.

'We need it more than they do. We will never get through these hills on foot.'

'We wait until it is dark?' said Kurylin.

'They will never let us alone that long, if they are still up there.' Galina sat with her sturdy knees up to her chin. The nervous tension had brought on a sudden thirst. They had water in the jeep – that dusty jeep was just about everything to them. Still they heard nothing. Not a trickle of a rolling stone.

There was no chance that the truck would come looking for them, not for some hours. Borlov had been the most experienced man in their team, and nobody would expect him to get lost. They would not be missed for a long time. They could see a stretch of the dusty track they had come along, some stunted trees and the rocks. Desolate and forbidding. Ideal for an ambush. Borlov was dead, his body hanging up there behind them, upside down in the sun.

'How long should we wait?' said Kurylin. 'We should be doing something.'

'Perhaps they have gone,' said Galina. 'They were not ordinary bandits, I think, or they would be coming down to steal the jeep by now. Those people will steal anything, it is an old tradition with them.'

'Without the jeep,' said Kurylin, 'we can do nothing. We should not have stopped here.'

'Borlov was in charge. He was not expecting to die here. They shoot accurately, and they can move very quietly.'

'There were two,' said Kurylin. 'I should have taken the gun when we stopped, I should have gone with Borlov, that would have been the sensible and correct thing to do.'

Galina hunched her shoulders. 'Then I think you would be dead as well.'

'So we sit here and do nothing?' Kurylin wiped the sweat from his forehead with his forearm.

'Have patience,' said Galina, 'there is yet time.'

They were huddled close together, whispering, like a pair of lovers. Borlov had been their first casualty, and they had met with so little trouble so far that they had been forgetting the possibility of sudden death.

They were both young, doing a job, the job they had been sent to do, and they had been amply warned of the dangers.

Galina watched the minute hand of her watch move slowly along, her arms wrapped round her knees. It was the middle of the afternoon, warm and airless under their protecting piece of rock. No room to move. Nowhere to go, except over to the jeep, their only salvation.

Nearly an hour went past, and there was still no sound above or anywhere near them. No breeze to cool them and dry the sweat that trickled down behind their ears and into their eyes and inside their shirts.

Kurylin shifted his stiffening legs. 'We have waited long enough. They are not there now. Be ready to run and come with me when I have the engine going.'

He crawled out from under the rock, got to his feet and began to run, bending over and swerving. He had taken a dozen steps when the first shot rang out, he staggered and threw up his arms and fell to his knees, the second shot came fast and flung him round so that Galina could see his face, the gaping mouth and the expression of surprise before he collapsed. She saw his hand outflung and twitching at the dirt. He lifted his head a little and the blood gushed out and down into the dirt. There was no more movement.

With blurred eyes she sat and watched the body. It seemed to have shrunk, to have flattened itself lower and lower. If he had stayed with her he would still be alive, for a little while longer. She could expect no more than that herself. He had a young wife and a little baby girl in Kiev. A good man.

She pushed herself out from the rock and stood upright and walked out into the sun slowly. She might as well die now and she braced herself for the impact of the bullet that would finish it quickly.

There was no shooting. She stood over Kurylin's body, knelt by it, and touched it softly, expecting to join him now, wishing there might be something in that old fashion of praying that had never been any part of her living. That old God-myth. Perhaps? Old people still took comfort from it when they knew they were nearing their end.

Scientifically it was absurd, of course. There could be no God. Could there?

Death was the end. She raised her head to shout at them up there to hurry and finish it, in a sudden burst of angry impotence.

She saw the two young men bounding over the rocks, with their rifles. Two thin, dark men, one of them bearded, quicker than the other. Both of them wore dirty shirts and tattered trousers, and they were as quick as monkeys over the steep rocks. Just two of them.

Too late she started to run over to the jeep, stumbling in her heavy boots. The one with the beard caught her easily and wrapped an arm around her neck, almost lifting her off her feet. He dragged her back, her boots scraping in the dust, and dropped her beside Kurylin's body.

His companion turned Kurylin's body over on to its back, using his toe, and spat into the dust. They both stared down at Galina, their eyes dark and expressionless, almost incurious.

She sat up carefully. They could easily have shot her before this. She must not show them how frightened she was.

In a thick guttural French they exchanged a few words, and she understood enough to know what was going to happen to her. The bearded one shoved her back with his foot and put his rifle down, and she kicked and fought as he reached down and tore her shirt away.

She managed to bite his hand, but he shifted too quickly for any of her wild kicking to do any damage, and his companion grabbed both of her hands and tugged them back behind her head and pinned them to the ground.

The bearded one squatted on her belly, whipped the remnants of her shirt away, and slapped her breasts with vicious long fingers, backwards and forwards until she screamed and bucked and failed to dislodge him.

They were serious and unsmiling, joyless celebrants to their own lusts. She was just a thing, a female thing. Foreign and inferior, and of no significance except to provide a temporary relief, mechanical and degrading.

They had stripped her, except for the high laced boots which they had no interest in removing. Coupling in the dust in the revealing sunlight beside a dead body, they both took her, turn and turn about, until she lost all awareness and wished only for the death that could not be long delayed now.

When they had done with her they squatted beside her and smoked the cigarettes they had found in her case. She was nothing any more, not even worth looking at, she had the smell of a foreign woman and her breasts were clumsy.

Yusuf was the one with a beard. He was not quite twenty, but he had been in Tangier and across to Marseilles, and thus reckoned himself vastly experienced about women. If the inclination returned he would have her again. So he was waiting. He had taken her watch, which had not been damaged in the struggle. It was a good one. Foreigners mostly had good things.

Mossou was almost eighteen, a bony youth who had been nowhere yet. If it had not been for Yusuf he would not have touched the woman, but then Yusuf would have made him a joke with the others, calling him Sister Mossou – frightened to be a real man.

The woman lay very still between them, her eyes shut against the sun, only her stomach lifting.

'I have had many better,' said Yusuf. 'She had no skill, this one – a foreign cow, we have been doing her an honour, little Mossou.'

Mossou scratched one dirty finger down the length of his sharp nose, which indicated he was thinking.

'We should leave her now. I have had enough. We give her the clothes. She can walk, and we take the jeep. That will be good.'

Yusuf grunted. 'You think like a fool.'

'Leave her. We cannot take her with us.'

Yusuf, still squatting, glanced sideways up at him. 'So she goes walking, perhaps she meets some of her people, and she tells what has happened to her – you think that will be good?'

Galina had opened her eyes, weeping in spite of herself. She rocked her head from side to side, and drew up her knees to hide some of her nakedness, trying not to make any sound.

Mossou stood up and went over to the jeep. He had driven one before. This would be a good trophy to take back with them. More vehicles were needed, especially one like this. He got in and ran the engine and it sounded very fine.

He heard Yusuf shout, and when he looked Yusuf was bending over the woman with his rifle against her head and his foot on her chest to keep her steady. When he fired there was a little jerk in the woman's body and there were echoes ringing around the hillside.

Yusuf shouted again, angrily, and beckoned him over. They had three bodies to arrange and Yusuf was not inclined to do it all himself while young Mossou sat like a girl in the jeep.

Yusuf towed the body of the woman in among the rocks. He thought of taking her boots, but they would be too small. He sent Mossou up the rocks to bring the body of the old one down, then they stripped the bodies of the men and jammed all three together in a crack in the rocks, with the woman underneath, which Yusuf remarked was the right place for her.

They collected some money, mostly French, and cigarettes. Yusuf emptied his bladder over the tangled corpses while Mossou backed the jeep on to the track. And they drove off.

Their meeting with the survey party had not been planned, and the ambush had been accidental. They had been on the way to a remote little dried-up water-course that snaked through the hills – goat country, arid and uninviting; scree and stunted bush; no way through for wheeled traffic, except perhaps a jeep in the hands of one who knew how to drive it properly, such as Mossou.

There were caves in the rocks, as old as the rocks, and easy to miss unless you knew where they were, and very few knew that. In the smallest cave there was a little stream that trickled down one wall and filtered out of sight into a crevasse so deep that nobody knew where it went, and the water was so cold that it chilled the teeth, but it seldom stopped flowing – icy water with the taste of iron in it.

Mossou ran the jeep in among some bushes where it would not readily be seen. It was a fine vehicle, the Russians had good transport. There was also the rifle and a packet of ammunition. The survey instruments meant nothing, so they were left. Yusuf broke off some branches and wiped out the marks of their wheels in the dust.

When he had done he slapped Mossou on the back. They had done well. He would do the talking. Agreed?

'You shot the woman,' said Mossou sourly. 'You tell Abu Hafidh what a great warrior you have been. I say nothing. I drive the jeep, you could not do that.'

'Any woman can drive,' said Yusuf loftily.

'It is nothing, little Mossou. I shot the old one on the hill, and that was good shooting.'

Mossou shrugged. 'It was not necessary. They would never have seen us.'

'Little fool,' said Yusuf, his voice indulgent. 'A gun is for shooting and they were the foreign pigs, now there are three less, so dry your tears.'

One day, Mossou thought, I will cut your liver out and feed it to the crows, son of a whore of a she-camel.

They clambered up the rocky slope to where the sentry waited for them squatting by a bush with his rifle across his knees. It was Burabin, Yusuf's cousin, a grown man who had in his youth worked in the tin mines at Meknes. An ill-tempered man, but the best rifle shot they had.

'You are late,' he growled. 'You should have been here two hours ago. Abu Hafidh does not wait for boys.'

'We have been busy,' said Yusuf.

'Busy fornicating.'

'A little,' said Yusuf. 'We have also shot three Russians and taken their vehicle.'

'I heard it,' said Burabin wryly. 'You would have been quieter on foot. The Russians must have been blind or drunk, or asleep perhaps? Or were they all women?'

'Only one,' said Yusuf.

Burabin waved them on contemptuously. 'She will have given you the pox. Go up and get your medals.'

Yusuf thought of many things to say, but said none of them, because it was never wise to provoke Burabin, and that evil temper of his was soon roused, cousin or no cousin.

That was why he had left the mines at Meknes, in a hurry, leaving behind him two work-mates and a foreman who would make no more ill-timed jests about peasants from the hills who were too stupid to know one end of a tool from another.

Nor were the police at Meknes the only ones who would be happy to have Burabin under lock and key: he no longer cared to appear publicly in Fez or Quezzane, for similar reasons.

So Yusuf swallowed his indignation, and they went on up to report to Abu Hafidh in the cave by the water.

FOUR

Abu Hafidh came from a poor family in Ahminad, one of many little removed from the poverty line, so there should have been no kind of future for him. But Abu was no ordinary boy: he was intelligent and alert and eager to learn, and invariably cheerful.

Richard Ahmin's English mother had picked young Abu out as an interesting youth and well worth helping; she had arranged for him to attend the high school in Marrakesh where his progress had been gratifying. Her own son, Richard, on holiday from his school in England, had made friends with Abu, and the two boys, so dissimilar in background and position, had always got on together very well.

Abu could ride anything that had four legs, barebacked and without bridle, and over the wildest countryside, and already he was an excellent shot with a .22. And all these exciting skills he was happy to teach Richard, since they were no part of the curriculum at his school in England.

In return Richard had taught Abu how to swim, which had not been all that simple because Ahminad had few suitable stretches of water, and they had to wait until Richard's mother Mildred could drive them down to the sea at Casablanca or Mohammedia.

As the boys grew older they naturally saw a little less of each other, but the friendship was there, and whenever Richard was in Ahminad Abu would be one of the first people he would go looking for.

Abu's ambition was to be a silversmith and jeweller, following the ancient craft of his people, making beautiful things – silver sugar basins, mint boxes, ceremonial trays, necklaces of heavy amber inlaid in silver, chiselled cosmetic boxes for ladies of fashion – all wrought in the austere dignity of a craft that went back over a thousand years.

Mildred Ahmin paid for Abu to be trained under a master silversmith in Tangier, and later made it possible for him to set up on his own in Ahminad. Abu's business prospered, and his wares were sought after by discriminating collectors. Among the younger business men of Ahminad he had become one to be reckoned with, as a fearless and outspoken critic of the way the affairs of Ahminad were being conducted by Hasman Ahmin and his clique of elderly sycophants and corrupt hangers-on – the survivors of a bygone age of privilege.

It was unwise of him and dangerous, but he was young and hot-blooded and full of ideas, an intelligent young man's ideas, and not all of them were too visionary ever to be real.

Hasman's ancient taxation machinery operated with arbitrary and crippling effect: edicts were issued on Hasman's name without discussion or consultation, the tax-payer either paid up or went out of business, and there was no court of appeal. If you happened to be in favour with Hasman and his entourage a handsome bribe in the right place might save you temporarily.

Abu Hafidh was one of the few who resolutely refused to pay round the back door for the privilege of earning a living. It was all very galling and frustrating to an ambitious craftsman who took a pride in his craft.

Mildred Ahmin's husband had died while on a visit to England. She had property in

England and Richard now was at Cambridge, so their visits to Ahminad had become less frequent in recent years, although they had kept in touch with Abu and knew something of the situation that had developed. Also, Hasman made it clear that their presence in Ahminad was not entirely welcome. They were intruders, Mildred Ahmin was a foreigner who had no business meddling in domestic matters and encouraging native workers to have notions about their station in life – such as Abu Hafidh.

As for Richard Ahmin, he was his mother's son. A playboy. Ahminad had no need for his kind. Harsh words had been exchanged, and not always in private. Hasman held the reins and he was going to crack the whip.

When his mother died after a short illness Richard paid what he expected to be his last visit to Ahminad. There were some family affairs to wind up. It was then that he fully realized what was happening, and what seemed likely to happen to the little country in the near future.

The Russian delegation had the inside track, and Hasman Abdullah Ahmin was in no mood to listen to any other point of view,

British or French. Russian teams of experts could be met with all over the place.

What had really decided Richard Ahmin to stay put and do something about the way things were going was the startling news that Abu Hafidh had been made bankrupt by a blatant piece of legal chicanery. Hasman Ahmin had resurrected an obscure ordinance which had made any business financed abroad liable to confiscation. Mildred Ahmin had been indubitably a foreigner, she had given Abu the capital to start his business, therefore Abu's business came under the ordinance, his stock was confiscated and the business closed.

Abu had escaped arrest by taking to the hills. Opposition to Hasman Ahmin was widespread but scattered, and quite without leadership. With a handful of followers and few resources, Abu had taken to the life his forefathers had known so well, that of a guerrilla fighter, although on a limited scale.

The arrival of Richard Ahmin provided the natural leader. He and Abu had had a number of secret meetings to plan some kind of a campaign while Richard still enjoyed some liberty of movement around Ahminad.

Richard had started cautiously enough,

with protest meetings and routine propaganda, trying to arouse public opinion and inject some spirit into its apathy, conscious all the time that he was walking a tight-rope.

He had been making progress, he thought. He had even been able to force some lengthy and stormy interviews with Hasman, during which insults had been tossed about and no kind of agreement reached. But he had made it clear to Cousin Hasman that he was heading for bigger trouble, and that very soon. The people of Ahminad were at last finding their voice, and Hasman would do well to listen to it.

Their final meeting had ended with Richard Ahmin escorted out of the Presence by an armed guard, with a warning that he should return to England forthwith, or else.

He had ignored the warning. Part of his authority with the opposition rested on his position as a man able to beard Hasman in his own residence without being afraid of him. For all his English blood and education, he was an Ahmin, and if it came to an eyeball-to-eyeball confrontation with Hasman he would never back down, and people were beginning to know that.

Unfortunately there was a small splinter-group who felt things were not moving fast enough, so there had been the sporadic attempts on Hasman's life, which had been no part of Richard's plan.

In the stampede that naturally followed, Richard Ahmin had waited around just too long, reluctant to see his peaceful campaign become a blood-bath, and unwilling to bolt for cover, as Abu had been pressing him to do.

So the result had been that he had lost his liberty of movement, and Colonel Tony Dimarco had arrived on the scene to make a bad situation infinitely worse. No longer would there be even the pretence of a rule of law. Dimarco was Hasman's creature, and discreet people in Ahminad would have to learn to keep their mouths shut.

From his hide-out in the hills Abu Hafidh had kept the resistance alive, but he needed supplies and he needed recruits, and most of all he had to know how things were in the town – with Richard Ahmin, for instance. He had set up an intelligence network of a sort, which kept him in touch with others who thought and felt as he did.

They might have been driven underground, but they were by no means beaten. Nor were they bandits out for plunder. The liberation of Richard Ahmin was their first priority, when they were strong enough to carry it off.

Abu knew the difference Dimarco had made, Richard now was being efficiently guarded, and to get him free would take good planning, military planning – a quick strike, a strategic diversion at the right time and in the right place to draw off the defences, then a rapid retreat with Richard Ahmin in their convoy. A military operation that could only be tried once. So it would have to work.

He had some of the men, good, quick shots who would not panic, men like Burabin, good men to have with you in a tight corner at night. Now he had to have the right kind of transport. So far they had been using two ponies, 'borrowed' by one of his group from a neighbouring landlord, which had been limiting their movements.

Thus the arrival of Yusuf and Mossou had been providential. He had known they were coming, but the jeep was a bonus. He listened to Yusuf's version of their exploit, and he knew there had been more to it than Yusuf was telling.

Abu himself had seen the Russian survey team passing along the roads once or twice, and he knew there had been a woman with them.

'And what did you do with the woman?' he said.

Yusuf spread both hands and turned the corners of his mouth down.

'What could we do, Abu? We could not let her go free.'

'We are not here to fight women,' said Abu. 'However, we did not invite her here. They are all safely put away?'

'Let the Russians look for them,' said Yusuf. 'There will be little left to find.'

'Good,' said Abu. 'Now go join the others, there is food if you are hungry. Mossou, I hear you are a good mechanic.'

'I drive anything,' said Mossou. 'The jeep has spare cans of gas – you wish me to drive you somewhere?'

'Tonight,' said Abu. 'It will be dangerous.'

'I drive you where you want to go,' said Mossou.

'Into the town when it is dark, and not by the roads?'

'With my eyes shut,' said Mossou.

'You are my man,' said Abu.

'It is the will of God.'

Mossou followed Yusuf into the large cave where the others squatted round a brazier.

Just six men with very little as yet but determination and a common cause. There was food, there were blankets, and a small assortment of weapons – the nucleus of a fighting force. Yusuf and Mossou were the youngest ones there.

Louise Vannier had flown into Rabat, there she had hired a Ford Escort Utility which she had driven herself over the dusty hills into Ahminad. There was no British consul, nobody from whom she could expect any kind of help. When people heard why she had come and what she wanted to do they became evasive and anxious to leave her company, which was not all that normal in her experience, especially with men.

She had looks and money and personality. So she went straight to the top.

Hasman had granted her one brief and unsatisfactory interview. He had been polite but adamant. Richard Ahmin was confined. He could see no outside visitors. None. Not even Louise Vannier who had come all that way on her own to see him.

Louise had pleaded to be allowed to send in a message. Surely that could do no harm?

'If you will give it to me I will ensure it reaches him,' said Hasman.

'Kind of you, but no thank you.' Louise's tone had been icy, and quite wasted on Hasman who had no regard at all for fair-haired European women, least of all this one who thought she had only to demand a thing and it would be done.

'This affair will not look good in the foreign Press,' Louise had said. 'It will draw attention to the mediaeval way you do things here.'

'If you had dared to say that to some of my predecessors they would have had the insolent tongue out of your mouth, and Richard Ahmin would have been chained in a dungeon.' Hasman had dismissed her and she had been unable to get at him again.

She had called at his Residence several times. She had been taken in across the courtyard and left in a gloomy waiting-room with the minimum of furniture. She had waited hours, in vain. A man-servant would at length appear. His Excellency was in conference with the Council of State, he would be unable to grant her an audience. Perhaps another day... His Excellency sent his profound regrets. Then she would be escorted out into the sunshine.

She had hung around the house where Richard was. The gates had remained locked and there were always armed guards, dumb and unco-operative except in the way they had looked her over, stripping her with their eyes.

She had tried telephoning from her hotel to people in London and Paris, people who might do something, but her calls always went wrong and in the end she guessed they were being interfered with. It was quite maddening.

And then that comic buffoon who called himself a Colonel had started to make a nuisance of himself, and everybody seemed scared of him and his gang in their fancy uniforms.

There just had to be some people who could help, if only she could get in touch with them, the men who hated Hasman's guts.

Early one evening she returned to her sitting-room in the hotel, and found there an uninvited visitor. Tony Dimarco wore a light blue suit and a white shirt, since he knew she didn't take his uniform or rank seriously, and he didn't want her to find this an amusing interview.

She halted in front of him and he didn't rise from his chair.

'Get out,' she said.

He pointed an unlit cigar at her and smiled. 'Don't get yourself steamed up, lady. We gotta talk a little, me and you.'

She was hot and tired. She was too weary to tolerate this oaf.

'Out,' she said. 'You have no business to be here.'

'You aiming to have me moved?'

She stalked over to the phone and rang down for the manager. Tony Dimarco sat there and lit his cigar while he listened.

The manager was apologetic and a little short of breath – and plainly embarrassed at her request to come up and toss Colonel Dimarco out of her rooms. He himself had let the Colonel in. It was a police matter, so she would please to understand that he was powerless. The Colonel had the authority and so on.

She slammed the phone down. Tony waved his cigar expansively. 'Don't blame the guy downstairs.' Beyond her he could see into her bedroom, he had already inspected it and he liked very much what he had seen. She wore nice stuff. Expensive. Plenty of taste. All those pricey perfumes, and she had her own private bath.

'Simmer down, lady,' he said. 'I go anywhere I like around here. You better believe that – save you some grief. I don't have to ask anybody.'

'Just an old-fashioned police state,' she said. 'How unpleasant for any decent people who still have to live here. You must have a hide like a rhino.'

He blew smoke over her head. 'I don't aim for popularity. I just like to keep an eye on things.' He smiled up at her. 'Suspicious characters and such-like.'

'There's a fool of a man who has been following me around,' she said. 'One of yours, I imagine?'

'For your own protection, lady. Too many rough characters around this place.'

'You must have a sense of humour,' she said, 'to sit there and talk such rubbish and expect me to listen. I don't want you here and I have nothing to say to you. Has that penetrated your thick skull?'

'I listen good,' said Tony Dimarco. She was the high-born lady addressing the ignorant peasant. Okay with Tony.

As she moved across the room the setting sun came through the slatted blind and shadowed her legs moving under her short skirt, and he knew he had to have her, somehow and somewhere, and then she would not be treating him like scum out of the gutter, by God no.

'I could help you,' he said, 'if you'd listen—'

She laughed, sharply, bitterly. 'You must be a comedian after all.'

'I could take you down to my office,' he said. 'It wouldn't be so funny, but you'd have to listen there, lady. I'd sooner keep it friendly.'

'You are having delusions,' she said. 'You and I could never be friends. You are a bandit in a silly uniform. So just go away and play policeman elsewhere.'

She sat down, picked up a magazine, and idly flipped the pages over. Some silent moments slid past. Tony Dimarco lounged in his chair, staring up at the ceiling where the smoke of his cigar swirled around the fan.

He was more aware of her than any woman he could remember. It had to be crazy, but she really got to him, and without looking her way he was seeing the long curve of her thighs, and he was imagining her in the bath over there and then waiting for him on that bed. All the night ahead of them.

She went on looking at her magazine, and the silence was building up between them.

She would have to make a move, and Tony

knew he could wait her out. She couldn't keep this up indefinitely. Then she would have to admit his presence, and listen to him.

When the phone rang he beat her to it. It was the manager, asking if everything was in order – and sorry he had spoken when he knew who was answering.

'Send up two bottles of whisky, Scotch, the best you got, and soda,' said Tony. 'Jump to it, boy.'

Louise Vannier tossed her magazine across to the settee.

'What are you planning?' she said. 'An orgy? That's not terribly original, even for you. You must do your drinking elsewhere, not here.'

'Richard Ahmin likes Scotch,' said Tony. 'Correct? We cut his liquor off, so I figured you might like to send him a little present.'

She just stared at him.

'No trick,' said Tony. 'He asked me to fix a bottle of hooch from Hasman, but I reckon it will come nicer from you, is that so crazy?'

There was a tap on the door and a nervous little coloured boy came in with a tray and the stuff. Tony pointed at the table. The boy put the tray down and backed smartly out of the room, having looked at neither of the occupants. Wise bar-boys knew better than to meddle with the Colonel, not when he had a white woman with him.

Tony opened one of the bottles and poured two drinks.

'Soda or neat?'

She didn't answer. Just went on looking at him, her blue eyes wary and hard. No party spirit. Only cautious hostility.

He put her drink, neat, on the table by her chair, and stood looking down at her. He could see the soft rise of her breasts.

He lifted his glass. 'To our better acquaintance.'

He had the toast all to himself. Her glass remained untouched. Her colour had heightened, just a little. But she kept her voice even.

'This is play-acting,' she said. 'You bore me, Dimarco. How does one insult a man like you? Do tell me.'

'You would like to visit Richard Ahmin?' he said. 'I can arrange it. Then you can take him the whisky. That is why I came here, to tell you this, and you talk of insults.'

'I don't believe it,' she said. 'Hasman Ahmin has repeatedly refused me permission to see him or send him a message.'

'It could be arranged.'

'What would you expect in return, Colonel Dimarco? Money? How much?'

'For a pretty girl you have an ugly mind,' he said.

'Perhaps it is the company I am obliged to keep. Is this a genuine offer?'

'You are here because of him,' said Tony Dimarco. 'So you should not be treating me like dirt.'

'And what about Hasman Ahmin? Aren't you supposed to be his private policeman?'

'The best they got, lady.'

'I wonder if I've been misjudging you,' she said slowly.

'The next time I come calling, you drink with me,' he said.

He finished his whisky, nodded at her, and strode out. That would start her guessing. Maybe have her thinking old Tony boy wasn't such a raw character after all, and that didn't have to be a bad move.

She sat looking at the bottles of whisky, puzzled, not at all easy, wondering how long he had been there before she came in. He would have snooped. Obviously.

She went through to her bedroom. The meeting had unsettled her. Colonel Tony Dimarco had been acting out of character.

So what did he hope to get out of it? As if she didn't know. Not just money. She had met her share of men like him.

She checked her luggage, including the small leather case with the little concealed pocket made for her by a craftsman who was specially good at that kind of thing, in Paris. The small automatic was still there.

Nothing had been disturbed, but she knew he had been in there.

Down in the hotel lobby Tony watched with approval as the nervous manager scuttled back into his office. It showed the right amount of respect for the colonel's rank and status. Keep the bastards jumping, the Dimarco motto.

Peter Piersson was the duty boy. A Swede with an engaging boyish face and thick, fair hair worn long, he had a consuming interest in some aspects of the female anatomy, like a prurient schoolboy who has just discovered that women are not made like men. Formerly a sailor, he had been with Dimarco for nearly two years, which made him one of the privileged veterans. He sat comfortably in the best chair in the lobby, studying the full-frontal and lasciviously contorted nudes in a privately printed magazine.

Tailing Louise Vannier around the place suited him fine, since it allowed him material to indulge in his favourite erotic fantasies during which the blonde would be at his mercy and he would perform prodigiously. It might even happen because he was a healthy boy and she knew he was right there wherever she went.

This was the first time the Colonel had been up there in her room with her. Lucky bastard.

'Okay, chief?' said Peter Piersson, bright-eyed and interested, man-to-man.

'That's right,' said Tony. No harm in letting it get about that the boss had made another score.

'Reckon she won't be going out anywhere tonight?' Peter Piersson said and grinned. 'Okay if I sign off later?'

'The job got too much for you?' said Tony. 'Don't strain yourself, boy.'

'Check,' said Peter Piersson. 'I'll stick around.'

'It's been a long, heavy day for the little lady as well,' said Tony.

'Sure,' said Peter Piersson. 'I didn't hear no screaming up there.'

Tony Dimarco patted him lightly on the shoulder. 'It's those pictures, they got you all stirred up.'

'Could be, chief.'

'She wouldn't give you the time of day,' said Tony. 'Forget it, kid.'

He walked masterfully out to where his car waited. He was the guy on top of the heap. But Peter Piersson called him a dirty name, under his breath.

Later on, with a brace of free drinks under his belt, Peter Piersson went upstairs and knocked at her door. Hell, he was a free man, wasn't he? And she was only another stray woman in a hotel room on her own.

If a crude pig like Tony Dimarco could get it, Peter Piersson argued that she ought to give him a proper welcome and do herself a real favour.

She opened the door just a little, saw who it was, and slammed the door before he could get a foot inside. He heard her turn the key, and in a couple of minutes that old git of a manager came steaming up and bleating and waving his hands around.

She had phoned a complaint and the manager was proposing to pass it along to Colonel Tony Dimarco, no less.

Peter Piersson smoothed him down. It had all been a little misunderstanding. The gallant manager planted himself in front of her door. Peter Piersson told him to get stuffed in Swedish, and drifted down to the lobby.

Louise Vannier did not appear, and her food went up on a tray. Peter Piersson wrote her off temporarily. A stupid cow.

FIVE

Several things happened in the course of the night. First of all, the matter of the missing survey team had become urgent, demanding investigation.

Lepelov was in charge of the Russian party, and he had waited long enough for the missing jeep to turn up. An incident of the kind reflected badly on a leader's reputation, and did not look well on his report, even though it had not been his fault. It was likely to be remembered when a man was being considered for another and a more important assignment. It was a crisis, and he would be judged on the way he had handled it.

Lepelov was in the early fifties, an efficient and skilful negotiator, with a good record for putting a job through. He looked the part. He was tall, still slim, with grey hair and a dignified bearing.

For the last few years his career had been marking time, and he had begun to think that he had reached his limit in the hierarchy – a middle-grade administrator, sound and unspectacular, with his best work behind him, almost ready for his pension.

There were the younger men pushing up, energetic and critical, trained in all the new technologies – diplomats and economists and engineers, traveling the world with soviet delegations, observing and reporting back, and all the while being groomed for promotion. The new breed.

In the face of such opposition, a man like Lepelov knew he could afford to make no mistakes. Otherwise the best he could hope for would be some obscure ministry appointment far removed from the areas where things happened and careers were advanced.

So Ahminad might be his last chance. He was not new to the Arab world. He had served in Egypt and Syria with distinction, as a senior member of the Soviet parties, and he was supposed to be good at finding his way through the involved intricacies of Arab politics.

From the start, Ahminad had presented difficulties. There had been the attempts on Hasman's life, prompted by his acceptance of the Russians in the country. Now a valued team of experts had failed to return – Russian experts. And a survey team just does not get itself lost. Not even in Ahminad.

Lepelov made a formal call on Hasman Ahmin in his Residence, and Hasman summoned Tony Dimarco to join the conference. Lepelov had brought with him the map of the district where his men had been working.

'An accident?' said Hasman. 'It is bad country up there. It is not difficult to miss the track.'

'Not for my men,' said Lepelov. 'They do not lose their way. There has been no storm, and all our vehicles are in excellent condition. Something has happened to them.'

Dimarco lit himself a cigar, neither of the others smoked.

'They'll show up in the morning,' he said. 'No panic. Two men and a woman. Sounds okay to me.'

Lepelov ignored him. 'I must ask for a search to be started, now, this night. Borlov is my most experienced surveyor, I cannot afford to lose him, or the others.'

'Colonel,' said Hasman, 'you will take some of your best men and see what you can find.'

'Now?' Tony grinned.

'Now,' said Hasman. 'You have a truck with a spotlight.'

'Need more than a light up there,' said Tony – 'That's rugged territory.'

'If anyone can find them you are the man, Colonel,' said Hasman.

'Seems like a waste of time to me,' said Tony. 'But if you say so we'll take a crack at it. Didn't those guys have any radio in their wagon?'

Hasman glanced at Lepelov.

'All our vehicles are equipped with radio when engaged on field work.' Lepelov directed his answer to Hasman, still refusing to recognize the presence of this clown masquerading as a military man. Nothing like this would ever be tolerated among Lepelov's people.

'So why haven't they called up base?' said Tony. 'I reckon that's a good question, don't you? You got any ideas?'

He had put the question to Lepelov deliberately, he wasn't going to have any Commie boss treating him like crap just because a bunch of his guys had gone missing.

'What in hell's the good of a radio if they don't use it? That's all I'm asking.'

80

Lepelov drew himself up, breathing noisily through his nose, and Tony went on grinning, waiting for the explosion.

Hasman intervened. 'Colonel,' he said, 'collect your men.'

Tony held out his hand. 'The map,' he said. 'We're not running all over the goddam mountains in the dark. Let's have a clue here and there – the route they were supposed to be on and where they were last seen and when.'

'It has been prepared. The map has been marked.'

Lepelov handed it over to Tony, neatly folded to show the area where the jeep had been traveling. Tony studied it for a moment. At least he had made this guy know he was in the room.

'Okay,' he said. 'We'll give it a try. Did they have any hardware with them? Guns?'

'All my teams are suitably armed when operating in the field.'

'Guns and a radio, hell,' said Tony, 'they should be okay.'

'Find them, Colonel,' said Hasman. 'Take whatever you think you need.'

Tony stuffed the folded map into his pocket and started for the door, still trailing smoke from his cigar. He was doing them a favour.

'What we need we don't have,' he said. 'Daylight and the use of a good chopper pilot. That's the only way to run a proper search up in those goddam hills.'

When he had left them, Lepelov said, 'you find that man trustworthy?'

'As long as I pay him,' said Hasman. 'And I pay him well. When he has served his purpose, it will be different.'

'It will need to be very different,' said Lepelov. 'I cannot afford to lose any more of my men. There must be stability here, or our joint plans will be thrown into jeopardy.'

Hasman's dark eyes glittered. These lectures from Lepelov on the internal instability in Ahminad were becoming more frequent. Lepelov had hinted more than once that his masters would be willing to draft into Ahminad their own security force – on their own conditions.

And Hasman knew very well what his own position would be if he let that happen – no more than a puppet. This affair of the missing survey team could not have happened at a worse time. They would be the first casualties among the Russians. And there might well be others very soon.

Tony Dimarco collected his posse. Their

truck had reinforced panels at the sides, bullet-proof tyres, a spot-light mounted on top of the cab, and an array of automatic weapons. There were five men, a driver, and the Colonel himself to lead the expedition into the wilderness. Since this was an irregular patrol outside their normal duty nobody was going to wear uniform, and the Colonel said that was okay with him as well.

His briefing had been received with some derision on the part of the troops – so somebody had knocked off a bunch of the Commies and their boss was wetting his pants over it. So what did those guys expect? The way they were running all over the place some of them had to get liquidated by the local boys.

'So we ride off and bring in the stiffs,' said Tony cheerfully. 'Maybe you guys will get a medal. Big deal all round. His Excellency has given us a vote of confidence.'

They told him what His Excellency could do with his vote, and climbed aboard.

Some hours later they were grinding up yet another defile, as featureless and inhospitable as all the others. Their spot-light showed nothing but rocks and grey scrub and a lousy surface not fit for wheeled traffic. Tony was in the front with the driver, checking the map; the men were in the back, smoking and grousing, because this was one hell of a way to pass the night, and everybody knew they weren't going to get any action.

There had been some speculation about the missing Russian woman, some of them had seen her and said she looked okay. Healthy and clean, which you couldn't say for many of the females around the place. Arab bints. Hell, she-goats smelt better.

A couple of times old Colonel Tony had stopped the truck and had them all tumbling out onto the road with weapons at the ready, like in the good old goddam army. Practice to keep the guys awake ... *hup-hup-hup ... down on your bellies and crawl you bastards...*

It was getting chilly up there. At least it was warmer inside the truck. Tony hadn't found a clue, they were turning back for home.

Abu Hafidh, with Mossou and Burabin, had been watching the truck down below for some time as it wound through the hair-pin bends at little more than a walking pace most of the time, the bright spot-light flickering around, searching among the rocks, the noise of its engine filling the valley. And they knew whose vehicle it was, up there so late, where few vehicles came even in daylight.

Mossou pointed down the slope. 'The bodies are down there, Abu. We put them among the rocks. They will see nothing. We left nothing down there and they are well hidden.'

'You should have moved them farther away,' said Abu.

He whispered something to Burabin who lay beside him with his rifle. The range lessened with each twist of the track. There were two headlamps and the spot-light, and a truck moving slowly.

Burabin edged carefully forward, and settled himself, cuddling his rifle, his breathing even and regular. The rifle had become part of himself, familiar and easy.

He waited until the right moment. The truck had straightened after a sharp turn, its triple lights were in front and below, eighty yards away and now beginning to speed up.

Burabin fired three times, so rapidly that they sounded like one and the echoes chased around the ravine. The two head-lamps were out, and the spot-light. Burabin collected the three spent cases: why leave evidence where he had been? Let them guess.

Abu tapped him on the back. It would have pleased him to stay and see how many of them he could pick off as they fell out of their truck down there. He slid back among the rocks as the sounds of confused activity came up from the track where the truck had lurched to a halt. He joined Abu and young Mossou, and they melted away, fast and silent.

'Before God,' said Burabin, 'I could have had them all, Abu.'

'We have a journey to make,' said Abu. 'Without lights they will not travel far, and the night is not yet over.'

They heard the heavy *thunk-thunk-thunk* of machine-gun, and a scattering of rifle fire. Then it all suddenly stopped, which meant that whoever was in command knew they were wasting ammunition.

Dimarco's men had spread out with the truck as a shelter while they tried to decide where that shooting had come from – which side of the rocks?

The machine-gun had sprayed bullets right and left, and two of the automatic rifles had added their crisp quota. Tony Dimarco and the driver slid down out of the cab and Tony squatted behind one of the wheels.

They had seen nothing, no flashes.

Just three shots. No more. Tony shouted a command. And waved his team forward to the foot of the rocks beside the track. There was no more shooting from up there. He could hear the whispering among his men, mostly profane admiration for the shooting – this was the kind of stunt they had pulled themselves so often in the past.

Tony shut them up. One guy or three of them up there? One, he thought. It had sounded like one. A guy who had the nerve to sit up there and take out their three lights had to be respected.

He examined what he could make out of the terrain. That Commie bastard would hoot like hell when he heard of this one – Tony Dimarco and his boys jumped by some ragged Arab in the hills, shot up and left to walk home.

He left the driver with the useless goddam truck, and the machine-gun, and he took his boys up among the rocks – and none of them was anxious to stick his head too high.

They slithered about for half an hour or so

with moderate enthusiasm, until Tony decided the mission had aborted and led them down again.

There was nothing to be done about the truck. They were stuck there until it was light enough to risk those curves, and there was no guarantee the sharp boy with a gun wouldn't come back and have a little more target practice, and old Colonel Tony was in a real mean mood.

No smoking and no talking; they had to arrange themselves in the rocks and keep out of sight and one guy had to do sentry go.

The driver fooled around with the shattered lights, trying to fix up something. But those bullets had made a real mess of the lamps, and he couldn't do anything.

Louise Vannier had been in bed for some hours. She was a healthy girl, and insomnia had never bothered her before; not until this trip to Ahminad. She was drowsy, half asleep, just waiting for sleep to take her off and set her mind at rest as well as her body.

She was suddenly aware that her bedroom door was opening slowly, and she lay there stiff and unmoving as she made out a dark figure coming in, a man.

88

Holding her breath, she pretended to be sleeping, her eyes half closed, and she watched the man close the door silently behind him. A burglar, a night prowler – she hadn't expected that here in the hotel.

He wasn't moving, after he had entered, and she could make out the shine in his eyes. He didn't seem to be carrying any weapon. He just waited like a dark shadow over against the wall by the door, and she found herself getting over her first fright. She was waiting for him to begin searching her room ... there were things on her dressing-table worth stealing, jewellery, money, more than enough to satisfy a thief.

As soon as he was busy over there she was going to slip out of bed and into the other room to raise the alarm. He didn't appear able to make up his mind. He didn't move. But he was watching her, and she thought he must know she wasn't asleep. If he moved towards the bed she was going to scream. All she had over her was a single sheet, and she had grasped one edge without realizing she had given herself away.

'Do not be frightened,' he said softly.

She sat up, reached for the bedside light and put it on. He wore a dark shirt and trousers, and he held up both hands to show her that they were empty. A very well-mannered and considerate burglar.

'Who are you?' she demanded. 'Don't come any nearer or I'll scream.'

'Please,' he said persuasively, not moving, 'make little noise, please – there is no need to scream. I am Abu Hafidh. Richard has spoken of me? Richard Ahmin?'

She stared at him. Richard had shown her pictures of him. He had been clean-shaven then, and a little younger. Richard's Arab friend and his mother's protégé.

She tilted the lamp so that she could see him better, and he smiled – a dark-bearded man with a strong nose and the look of a natural-born adventurer about him.

'Yes,' she said quietly, 'I recognize you, Abu Hafidh. I didn't expect to meet you like this – I thought you were a burglar.'

She reached for her wrap and got out of bed.

'The light,' he whispered. 'It should be out. It may be noticed.'

She switched the light off and sat on the edge of the bed. 'How did you get in here? The door was locked.'

'One of the hotel servants,' he murmured. 'We still have useful friends here ... there was no other way to speak with you. I am

90

glad you had the courage not to shout – I did my best not to alarm you too much. I have a message from Richard, for you–'

'How is he?' she said quickly.

'He remains well.'

'I've tried to see him,' she said.

'He knows that. He wishes you not to take any more risks–'

'–I've done nothing – I haven't been able to do a thing!'

He put a finger to his lips, drifted over to the window, and looked out through the blinds down at the ornamental gardens. They were on the first floor, in the front of the hotel, a vulnerable position if he had to leave in a hurry. He had come in through the servants' quarters, and Burabin waited for him there by the stables. They had left Mossou with the jeep outside the town, well hidden.

It was two o'clock in the morning, and the main avenue was quiet. Since the arrival of Tony Dimarco and his gunmen there was little traffic at night. Discreet citizens remained at home after dark.

Abu went back to Louise. 'We can get a message through to Richard, there is an old gardener who works in the grounds still, he used to work for Richard's mother, we are able to keep in touch through him.'

'Would a letter be too dangerous? I'd like to write to Richard.'

'Richard would like that. But he says he would like you to leave here, Miss Louise – this is not a good place for you now.'

'Not very good for Richard, either,' she said. 'He's a prisoner, at least I'm free to move about, even if I don't manage to achieve anything useful. I'm not leaving, Abu, and to hell with Hasman Ahmin and that thug of his – they make a lovely pair.'

'I hear you had a visit from Dimarco,' said Abu. 'It was not pleasant?'

'No,' she said. 'I wouldn't trust him. I find his kind of man quite poisonous – he is stupid and vicious.'

Abu allowed himself a tiny smile at the vehemence in her voice. 'You may be happy to know that Dimarco and some of his men are spending the night in a truck stranded up in the hills, there was an accident to the truck – somebody shot the lights out and they cannot drive it.'

Louise smiled at him. 'I imagine you were in the neighbourhood, Abu. Richard always said you were very good with a gun.'

'Not this time,' said Abu. 'It was a comrade of mine. I am regretting now that I did not let him try Dimarco as a target, but by then there was no light, and I thought it wiser to move on.'

'What is going to be the end of all this?' she said. 'It's such a little place and it's full of violence.'

Abu shrugged. 'Ask Hasman Ahmin.'

'You're going to beat him, aren't you? You have to, Abu … otherwise there can't be any sense to all of this.'

'I live as a fugitive,' he said. 'It is not my choice. There are many like me, but we need organizing … most of all we need a leader.'

'Richard is a prisoner,' she said softly. 'You should not look to him, Abu. He is in sufficient danger.'

Abu was silent for a while and his silence was like a reproach. This was a decision Richard would have to make for himself, and she thought he had already made it. She was just the woman who loved him, her only reason for being in Ahminad was to get him free of it. Abu was the last man she should talk to about danger. He was risking his life just by being there with her.

'You should not upset yourself,' he said. Although he could see little of her expression he knew what she was feeling.

'What can you hope to do?' she said. 'Are

you expecting to start a revolution?'

'We are doing what is in our power,' he said. 'Perhaps it appears very little – you may be hearing tomorrow of some Russian people who cannot be found, a road survey team. It will embarrass Hasman as well as the Russians. The Russians will not like losing their people, they will blame Hasman for not keeping the country under control, and that will work to our advantage eventually. It will take time.'

'You have not been idle,' she said. 'Those missing Russians, have they been killed?'

'Two young men who have just joined me,' said Abu, 'they caught them near where we stopped Dimarco tonight. If I had been there with them I do not think I would have stopped the shooting – we have no love for the Russians, they should not be here.'

'This is going to make a bad situation even worse,' she said. 'You realize that, Abu?'

'I am remembering a saying Richard used when we were boys here together – about breaking eggs to make an omelet.'

'More killing,' she said.

'It would be better if you went away,' he said. 'There are good hotels in Casablanca. It would make Richard happy to know you were there. Or Tangier.'

'No,' she said.

'It would be better,' he repeated.

'I didn't come here just to run away when things got difficult. I'm staying, Abu. They won't do anything to Richard, will they? Hasman wouldn't dare, would he?'

'Could you hope to stop him?' Abu's voice was flat.

'I'd do something,' she said. 'I wouldn't sit around a hotel and just let it happen.'

'Richard has made his position clear,' said Abu. 'He feels about the Russians being here as most of us feel, which is why Hasman is keeping him in the house and under guard. If we must have outside help to become prosperous and modern we would rather have the British, or even the French. Ahminad has become a football and the Russians are kicking with Hasman on their side … there are many of us who do not wish to continue as spectators. It is our country and our problem and we will solve it for ourselves.'

'I'm staying,' she said.

'Miss Louise,' said Abu, 'this will not be a business for women.'

'It will be, for this one,' she said. 'Hasman can throw me into jail, if he finds me a nuisance, but I'm not leaving on my own.

When I go Richard will be with me. Has-man is living in the wrong century.'

'Richard's mother used to tell him that often enough, Miss Louise. She also was a woman of courage.'

'You must be making some kind of plans to get Richard free?' she said.

'We are,' said Abu.

Impulsively she placed both hands on his shoulders. 'Richard was always right about you, and I am glad I know you at last.'

'My privilege,' said Abu softly. 'Now you will write the message for Richard. I should be going soon.'

She went into her sitting-room, groped around and found her lighter. She sat at her writing table and by the tiny flame wrote a brief note:

Darling Richard I love you and I'm not going to let Hasman drive me away. You won't be there much longer. Keep well and bless you.

Louise.

She folded the note very small. She thought about sealing it into an envelope, but she knew Abu wouldn't read it and he might take an envelope as an insult. The gardener probably could not read English, and a folded note would be easier to smuggle in than an envelope.

Abu stood in the doorway, watching her. She held out the note and he slipped it into a pocket.

'Richard will have it in the morning,' he said. 'It will cheer him.'

'Thank you, Abu. I feel better myself as well.'

'You know you are being followed?' he said.

'I do.'

'It would be wise not to go driving too far on your own,' he said. 'Into the country too far. I will come here again when I can. Go with God, Miss Louise.'

He left so quickly and so quietly that she heard nothing, not even the door closing. She went into her bedroom and lay on the bed and thought of all the things she should have put in the note to Richard. Abu Hafidh inspired confidence somehow, but she hoped he knew what he was about because to her the immediate future looked grim indeed.

SIX

A grey dawn was about to come up over the unsmiling hills. The light was nearly good enough to drive by, and the marooned party was already aboard in no very soldierly fashion because this surely hadn't been one of the exploits they would want to talk about much. Morale was low. They had been made to look foolish, goddam foolish like a bunch of novices, squatting there all night waiting for what never came.

It was the driver who spotted it after he had driven less than a hundred yards. A flock of vultures flapping about up in the rocks and tearing at something out of sight. Scrapping and shoving each other about, the way they always did over a good meal. Probably some goat come to grief up there.

The driver glanced at Tony, and Tony motioned to him to stop, pulled out his revolver and loosed off a couple of shots that sent the vultures skittering around. They didn't go too far, most of them settled again and made dirty bubbling noises, twitching their skinny necks indignantly. They didn't look good in the poor light. And soon they were hopping down the rocks to where they had been.

Tony swore and got out of the truck. This was a familiar scene in the jungle. He slapped the side of the truck and told them to tumble out, and he was among the rocks and smelling the odour he knew too well even when he was still yards away.

He emptied his revolver and the scavengers moved off in a flurry now, and a couple of his men were right behind him and saw what he was seeing stuffed down there among the rocks...

'Two guys ... there's a woman underneath, boss ... see her hair – kind of yukky, ain't it?'

'Musta been there all night and we never knew ... this the lot we been looking for, Colonel? I seen prettier sights, that's for sure ... funny how them bastard birds always go for the eyes first...'

The rest of the party joined them, including the driver and he spewed at the first glance and retired. Some of the others heaved rocks at the waiting vultures. It wasn't worth wasting slugs. Minute by minute the light was improving up there, and Tony Dimarco, who had a stronger stomach than most, knelt on the edge of the rocks and took a good long look at what was down there. But the bodies had been so torn about and mutilated that he couldn't see any signs of bullet wounds. All he could guess was that they had been there some time, and that they were what he had been sent to find.

The sight of the dead bodies didn't affect him, he had seen worse, but what did annoy him was the knowledge that the stiffs had been stuck there all the night within spitting distance of where he and the boys had been shot up – which meant that these chunks of rock weren't healthy … there must be one or two guys up there who could handle a gun. No fooling.

'We oughta pick them up and take them back with us,' he said. 'Kind of proof.'

The suggestion met with little favour.

'You gotta be joking, Colonel…'

'Catch me riding with that lot in the back…'

'Hell, they'd fall apart soon as we touched them – sooner walk and that's a fact…'

'Listen, boss, we found them didn't we? Ain't that what we came for? Ain't our fault they ain't fit to be moved, and we got nothing to wrap them in, for God's sake...'

'Okay, okay,' said Tony testily. 'I never seen such a bunch of sissies. But we ought to cover them up properly so those goddam birds don't get at them, and some of you fussy guys, you better scout round and see what happened to their clothes – if that don't scare you too much, you lazy bastards.'

He watched them scatter over the hillside and poke about in the rocks in a perfunctory fashion. There was the missing jeep, of course, but the sharp guys who had plugged the Russians and stripped them wouldn't have left the jeep around. It looked like a fair bit of military planning by somebody, and the more he thought about it the less he liked it.

The rebels had been a joke so far. Lousy shots and noisy talkers. But here was one little mob who could handle themselves.

He made a mark on the map he had got from Lepelov. If the Russians wanted a proper funeral and all that stuff they could come up here and do it for themselves. Maybe they'd get themselves shot in the ass as well.

He lit a cigar but it was too much that early in the morning and on an empty stomach, so he tossed it aside and whistled his reluctant warriors back. They had found nothing.

The vultures had returned to slither among the piled rocks, but they couldn't reach anything now. The truck finally moved off. The Colonel was in a grim bitching mood, and the boys in the back were subdued, there was nothing to celebrate. This was going to make them look real stupid as soon as it got spread around the place, taken for a bunch of suckers like that. Some battle for God's sake.

When they reached town Tony Dimarco found a messenger waiting for him, from His Excellency – he had been waiting most of the night after frequent phone calls to the Colonel's quarters had failed to bring any information.

Tony needed a shower and a shave and some chow, and he told the messenger to get the hell out of it. The messenger was insistent – His Excellency had given strict orders, he was to bring the Colonel as soon as he returned.

So Tony went, just as he was, no longer the blue-eyed boy. Not even a cup of coffee.

Hasman Ahmin was up and waiting with

nothing on his desk. His face was dark and saturnine and not overly friendly. Like a judge who had already made up his mind about the verdict.

So Tony jumped right in first.

'We found the Russians,' he said. 'All dead.' He slapped Lepelov's map down onto the desk. 'There. Stuck in the rocks, all three of them, been there since some time yesterday, I reckon. Must have been a smart ambush. Nothing else up there, no vehicle.'

'That occupied you all night, Colonel?'

'We ran into an ambush ourselves.'

'Casualties?'

'None, we were too quick.'

'So. Not a very effective operation – you took no prisoners? And you suffered no casualties?'

'Like I told you,' said Tony. 'They tried to jump us–'

'–How many were there, Colonel? We must know that.'

'They were scattered around up there,' said Tony easily. 'They busted our lights or we should have been back hours ago. There was some good shooting so we had to keep our heads down. I reckon we did pretty good.'

Hasman stared at him, his dark eyes

expressionless. 'You have all returned un-harmed. That does not suggest very good shooting on the part of the enemy, and you say it was an ambush. I do not get the picture clear in my mind, Colonel. Surely you wounded some of them?'

'Didn't find any. I reckon they must have taken them with them when they bolted over the hills.'

'And that took all night?'

Tony leaned forward on Hasman's desk. 'Okay, Excellency, say what's on your mind. You shoulda been up there dodging some of the slugs flying about in the dark, it wasn't any picnic.'

'That is what I pay you for, you and your men.'

'Sorry we got no corpses to satisfy you.'

'You are being impertinent,' said Hasman.

'Anybody can run into an ambush up there.'

'Evidently, Colonel. You have the Russian bodies with you? How did they die? I must inform Lepelov.' Hasman was reaching for the phone.

'We had to leave them up there,' said Tony. 'They been stripped and they were kind of messy. We don't mind having to shove stiffs under, but the birds had got at this lot and there was only the one truck, so we covered them.'

'Lepelov will not like that,' said Hasman.

Tony hunched his shoulders. The worst was over. He had put his story across and it was going to be okay, it was going to stick.

'Too bad,' he said.

'Lepelov will expect something better,' said Hasman. 'They were his people.'

'They musta run into more than they could handle,' said Tony. 'What was left didn't look so good, but if those Commies want to bury the poor bastards they'll need a bulldozer to dig them out, you got my word for that.'

'I doubt if that will satisfy Lepelov,' said Hasman.

'He can't do much about it,' said Tony. 'Those boys who jumped us, they had us pinned down real tight – they got some good organizing going for them, the best I've seen around here – there's a guy who knows the score.'

Hasman glanced up at him. 'That will be Abu Hafidh,' he said. 'We have spoken of him before.'

'He's a sight smarter than the others,' said Tony. 'Might be a pleasure to tangle with him sometime when he don't have the drop on us.'

'He is a guerrilla, as you are yourself, colonel.' Hasman's voice was thin. 'If you could search him out and deal with him you would earn more than my gratitude.'

Tony smiled. That was better. Last night's foul-up didn't count any more. Hasman still needed him – and Hasman was just a little worried about this Abu feller, that stuck out a mile.

'I reckon we just might handle him,' said Tony.

'You have already seen how elusive he is, Colonel, and he knows his territory.' Hasman drew a circle on the map, not a small circle, it took in plenty of ground, rough ground, none of it easy.

'As far as we know, he will be somewhere in there, Colonel, and he has a few men with him–'

'–He's got enough to be a goddam nuisance,' said Tony. 'I'd trade some of my layabouts for guys who can shoot that good. If you really want me to go out after him, it'll take plenty of preparation – that's rugged country up there.'

'This is your kind of fighting, Colonel.'

'That's right,' said Tony. 'So I see the snags. Right? This Abu feller is smart and he's tricky and he's operating on his own ground, so we have to figure all the angles–'

'–You plan your campaign,' said Hasman, a little impatiently. 'That is your business. I will support you. The day you bring me proof that Abu Hafidh is no longer of importance, that day will be a profitable one for you, Colonel.'

'Like him dead?' said Tony. 'Guys like him don't get taken prisoner.'

Hasman opened one slim, brown hand on the desk between them, then clenched it tight.

'The guy's as good as dead.'

'Just show me the body, Colonel. If he is dead you will have saved me trouble. Just remember he is an intelligent man, and resourceful. I want him removed before he troubles me further.'

'I get the message,' said Tony. 'Loud and clear.'

'There are some ignorant fools on the other side,' said Hasman. 'Abu Hafidh is not one of them. He could prove dangerous – he outwitted you, Colonel, and you are a professional fighter.'

'He picked his spot,' said Tony. 'Maybe I'll pick it next time and I'll be laughing.'

'I sincerely hope so. His success last night

will have encouraged him, it will bring him recruits, and he is likely to become a serious irritation.'

'I'm putting myself in this Abu's place,' said Tony. 'The first thing I'd be after, soon as I felt strong enough, I'd spring Richard Ahmin – there's a big connection there, right? They could use Richard Ahmin. If Abu broke him out then I figure you'd have real trouble.'

'I will have Richard Ahmin moved into the jail this morning,' said Hasman. 'It should have been done before.'

'I wouldn't do that,' said Tony. 'Abu Hafidh may have plenty of nerve, but he isn't going to try to bust his way into your jail. That would take more hardware than he's likely to have for a long time. You leave Richard Ahmin in the house where he is, then maybe Abu will take a chance on it one night – and that's when I'll have the drop on him for sure.'

'You would advise that?' Hasman sounded only half convinced.

'I'll get it all figured out before tonight,' said Tony. 'Right now Abu Hafidh feels good. He's knocked off those Russians. He made monkeys out of me and my lot. Okay. He's got it all going for him, and we have the red faces. So one night, pretty soon I reckon, he comes in to lift Richard Ahmin – and we give him the chopper.'

'It will not be as simple as that,' said Hasman.

'Give me time to kick the details around,' said Tony.

'Come and see me this afternoon,' said Hasman. 'There must be no mistakes this time, Colonel. Richard Ahmin and Abu Hafidh would make a combination I do not care to think about.'

'You're right there.' Tony Dimarco showed his strong yellowing teeth. 'With those two on the loose it wouldn't be healthy. But I got the right boys, and we'll sew it up right. Are you figuring to do anything about this Louise Vannier? She's part of the picture.'

'I could have her car confiscated, that would restrict her,' said Hasman. 'I am refusing to see her again. I have thought of sending her out of the country.'

'I'd leave her alone,' said Tony. 'We can use her as part of the bait – as long as she floats around here and acts the angry little lady she don't hurt anybody, and sometime Abu will want to contact her. That makes sense, right?'

'I will leave her a little longer,' said

Hasman. 'She does not embarrass me. Now I must deal with Lepelov. I would like it better if I could assure him you had killed some of those rebels last night.'

'Tell him to stick around,' said Tony. 'We ain't finished yet by a long way.'

'A poor beginning,' said Hasman.

Tony stared at him, then decided to smile it off. 'It was tricky,' he said. 'That's all. Nothing to shout about.'

'Lepelov will wish to see the place where it happened. It will be expected in his report.'

'I'll have one of my boys standing by,' said Tony. 'Maybe they'll get shot up as well. Okay if I go and clean up now?'

Hasman nodded and picked up the phone. Lepelov would be difficult. He would want to wave that big Russian stick of his. He would talk about compensation and retribution, and so forth.

Lepelov did all of that, in an icily controlled manner, and Hasman Abdullah Ahmin was suavity itself. It was an even match and it lasted over an hour. Lepelov wanted the bodies brought back for burial, of course.

They reached a compromise. Hasman undertook to send some labourers with the party, suitably equipped. Lepelov should judge for himself on the spot what was to be done.

Lepelov demanded an armed guard. Hasman agreed after some wrangling: a Captain and some men, they would not be Dimarco's men, and they would be of little use but Lepelov would not have to know that. They would be soldiers in uniform with guns, so it would look correct and proper.

Lepelov was eventually satisfied. Hasman saw him off the premises with inward relief and repeated expressions of regret at this dastardly outrage and assurances that the assassins would be speedily brought to justice. Perhaps Lepelov believed him.

In his requisitioned quarters, Tony Dimarco shaved and showered and sent his orderly for food. Louise Vannier had been on his mind, so he sent his orderly for the balance of his home comforts to set the day up right.

Elvira was doe-eyed and slender as a wand, except for her hard little breasts. She was virginal and shy and just over sixteen. She had parted with her virginity when she was twelve, and her shyness vanished the moment she wrapped herself round a man in bed. There was nothing that kid didn't know about sex and pleasing a man in bed.

Tony had picked her up a couple of days before, dancing in one of the native joints with spangles round her little belly and not much else and he had been keeping her handy and busy ever since, except last night. He hadn't paid her anything, and she had too much savvy to ask, just yet. The Colonel was the Colonel, and he could make life difficult for a girl who entertained in public.

So Elvira sidled into Tony's room, shucked off her few clothes with professional dexterity, and posed and stretched in front of him, and that in itself was a minor piece of eroticism. There was a faint sheen on her lithe body and the timeless odour of sandalwood. Lipstick on her breasts. And the sideways smile.

Tony stubbed his cigar.

'Over here, baby – quit shaking it about. I got work to do.'

Elvira knelt beside him on the bed, tugged at the dark hairs on his chest, pouting.

'You love Elvira, hey? We make nice jig-a-jig now?'

'You got the idea,' said Tony, and pulled her down beside him.

Elvira giggled, a little-girl giggle which was not appropriate in view of what he was doing to her.

'I hear men shooting at you last night,' she said. 'Everybody talking.'

'They missed,' said Tony. 'See for yourself, baby … that feel like a dead man to you?'

'Big, strong feller … yes man!'

'So don't talk so much,' said Tony.

He was feeling a heap better when he dismissed her. Some kid. Good as a tonic. Then he slept a little. Nothing like it.

Aziz, the elderly gardener, was not as deaf as he liked people to think – it simplified life and saved him the bother of having to reply to silly talk. The guards also thought he was not too bright. Just an old brown bastard with a face like a monkey. Thick as mahogany. Kick him in the ass and he'll fall to pieces – nothing there but skin and old bones.

Aziz shuffled past the guard with his basket of flowers, bringing with him his characteristic fertilizer smell. Nobody stopped him and nobody searched him. Hell, he was rank and stupid. Who needed flowers, for God's sake.

Aziz pressed the flowers into Richard Ahmin's hand, bowed and retreated, taking the empty basket. It had been fruit before, and the message would be tucked under the neatly cut rind of citrus or orange. Now flowers, with the message hidden among the stems.

Richard Ahmin smiled as he read it. He had tried to persuade her to stay away, and he had been waiting for this note from her. It meant that Abu had been in the town last night.

He had overheard the talk among the guards in the grounds – there had clearly been some excitement last night, an encounter in the hills involving Tony Dimarco and from which Colonel Dimarco had evidently not emerged with much credit.

When later Richard proposed to saunter forth into the sunshine and take the morning air he found the exit blocked by Lieutenant Prystocki from Posnan, Dimarco's trigger-happy Pole. Prystocki grinned and shook his head.

'No can do. New orders. You stay inside, boss. The garden is off limits.'

'Any special reason, Lieutenant?' said Richard pleasantly.

'Been some action,' said Prystocki. 'Everybody kind of nervous. It won't last. Until then you gotta stay inside.'

Richard glanced out over the sunlit garden.

Aziz was in his customary pose, bending over a flower bed, motionless as though in prayer. There was no chance of slipping him the note he had written for Louise.

'Lieutenant,' he said, 'would you ask old Aziz over there to bring me in a couple of fresh limes, there's a good chap.'

'I'll fetch them myself,' said Prystocki. 'No trouble. You can fix both of us a drink. Okay? My orders don't say I have to stay outside and sweat.'

So that was that. There would have to be another time, tomorrow morning, perhaps. Aziz would surely find another excuse for coming into the house.

Prystocki came in with the limes. He took off his cap and made himself at ease while Richard Ahmin got the drinks ready. It was an unusual situation, the prisoner playing host to his jailer.

Prystocki accepted a cigar. 'You hear the Russians lost one of their outfits yesterday? Two fellers and a girl, rubbed out up in the hills.'

'To be regretted,' said Richard, 'but not unexpected.'

'It's got the Commie boss stirred up all right. What I hear, he's been tossing some heavy talk around, and old Hasman isn't

115

laughing much, either. They figure this Abu feller fixed it.'

'Could be,' said Richard.

'Trouble ahead,' said Prystocki.

'A vale of tears. How is the Colonel bearing up?'

'Marking time. He's smart.'

'My own impression,' said Richard. 'I take it you are not a fellow-traveller, Lieutenant?'

'Me?' said Prystocki. 'I'll tell you how it is with me and them – you tie me up in a sack with a Russian and I'll tell you who comes out first – Casimir Prystocki, that's who.'

'I had a similar discussion with Colonel Dimarco. He also has a low opinion of politics.'

'Like I said, he's smart. If this Abu character knocks off the Russians one by one that's okay with me – I still got a job to do around here, so don't think you can start anything, check?'

'Check.' Richard Ahmin smiled.

Prystocki stood up, put on his cap and patted his holster.

'All squared away? Thanks for the drink – and keep your head down.'

In the course of the afternoon Richard saw Tony Dimarco walking about the grounds with Lieutenant Prystocki, busy over some discussion that seemed to be of a military nature. The Colonel was in full uniform, and if he had been carrying a swagger cane he would have been the picture of a smart Sandhurst product. Except for those bogus medal ribbons. Strategic dialogue was taking place, the waving of arms hither and thither. All highly entertaining to the observer.

Then they went up on to the flat roof, where the water tanks were, and Richard Ahmin was pretty sure they were not discussing his water supply.

A party of men arrived, Dimarco's own men. They carried a machine-gun and lots of bits of gear. They also mounted up to the roof. There was stamping about up there and some military cussing, from Colonel Tony Dimarco.

The house was evidently being got ready for battle. Very interesting. A machine-gun post on the roof. Richard waited for Dimarco to come in. There was the matter of ten thousand dollars they had discussed at their last meeting. Perhaps Dimarco had changed his mind. If anybody now tried to break into the house there would be heavy casualties.

Taking advantage of all the operational patter going on up above, Aziz crept in by the kitchen door, with vegetables. Richard Ahmin grabbed him by his skinny arm and pointed upwards.

'Tell Abu, soon as you can?' he whispered. 'A gun on the roof...'

Aziz nodded. His deafness had miraculously disappeared. He nodded, mumbled something about sons-of-pigs, and shuffled off out. Richard could only hope that the message would get through in time to stop a disaster. Abu was good, but he couldn't expect to cope against a machine-gun in the hands of men who knew how to use it.

Dimarco left the grounds without calling in, although he must have been aware that Richard had been watching him through the windows and from the front door. Then a truck backed in through the gates, and a busy bunch of men rolled cables and portable lights up on to the roof.

Lieutenant Prystocki supervised all this, and it was some time before Richard could get a word with him.

'Are you expecting an invasion, Lieutenant?' he asked politely.

'Anybody tries to come over the wall,' said Prystocki, 'there won't be enough to bury, we got lights up there to cover every inch of the wall.'

'I feel flattered,' said Richard. 'I hope none of my friends will come calling.'

'I got my money on Abu,' said Prystocki. 'He'll show up one of these nights when he reckons it's all nice and peaceful – then bam-bam and good night Abu.'

'You convince me,' said Richard.

'Any night you hear shooting,' said Prystocki, 'you be sure you wind your neck in, don't you go snooping out there.'

'I wouldn't dream of it,' said Richard Ahmin.

SEVEN

It was dark when Saadi was admitted into the Residence by a private entrance that few people knew of or were permitted to use. Saadi was a small, slight man, insignificant in his dingy *djellaba*, a sideways furtive looker, obsequious to his superiors and merciless to those who owed him money or had the misfortune to work for him.

He owned a number of properties in the town, including an establishment called, predictably, *The Oasis*, which offered the expected range of native dishes and allied entertainments. It was only moderately prosperous, since the tourist trade in Ahminad had fallen off in recent years, and the local patrons understood the fine art of making a *atai benaana*, mint tea, last a long time while the belly-dancers went through their business largely unregarded.

Tony Dimarco's Elvira had been one of the team, a profitable investment for Saadi who still hoped to extract some kind of a return from the Colonel for the use of his property. Permission to stay open longer than rival establishments and freedom from police interference would be most acceptable.

Saadi was no ordinary man of business. He had been functioning in effect as Hasman Ahmin's secret police. He had the aptitude and the mode of life that made him very valuable to Hasman, and very little happened that he didn't get to know about very soon.

He maintained a small army of informants, male and female, most of them in the kind of occupation where they could pick up bits and pieces of news from indiscreet talkers: waiters, maids, house-boys, market traders.

He paid them modestly, and very few of them ever had the nerve or enterprise to feed Saadi bogus information, because he could be a very unfriendly man with a long memory, and most of his informants were under some kind of an obligation to Saadi, such as money they could not afford to repay.

He was left to wait in a dimly lit corner near the domestic area, where the servants had the good sense to ignore his presence, although all of them knew who he was and what his business was. Widely disliked and even more widely avoided by the underlings, that was Saadi.

When at last he was ushered into the Presence he was left to stand by the wall unregarded and in the shadows, while Hasman went on with whatever he was doing with the papers on his desk. They had played this scene many times before, and Saadi would have been disappointed and vaguely disturbed if it had gone differently.

Eventually Hasman beckoned him to come forward into the pool of light by the desk, stared at him as though he had never seen him before, and said quietly, 'talk now.'

'*Inch-Allah*, if God wills,' said Saadi, 'I tell you all I hear – they are laughing at the Colonel, they say Abu Hafidh has made a donkey of the Colonel up in the hills, they wonder you give money to such a one. There is much talking in the *souk*, and it is not to the honour of Your Excellency–'

'–I am well able to guard my own honour,' said Hasman.

'I but report what I am hearing and what is being brought to me, Excellency. There is much foolish talking. Business is bad, the visitors are few and they spend little. So people talk. They were frightened of the

Colonel at first – now he is a joke with them–'

'They would do well to take him seriously,' said Hasman. 'He acts with my authority. I think the time has come for the Colonel to teach those talkers in the *souk* – and elsewhere – that they work only by my permission. Perhaps I will have the markets closed.'

Saadi lifted one narrow shoulder. 'The people will then starve, Excellency.'

'Should that grieve me? If they offend they must be punished. I will think about it further. You have more for me?'

'A rumour. It may not be true. They are saying Abu Hafidh was here in the town last night.'

'So. He was seen?'

Saadi shoveled the air with one hand, pouting. 'I have talked with none who say they saw him, Excellency.'

'A rumour. Do you believe it?'

'I do.'

'Are you an old woman?' said Hasman. 'Do you choose to believe all you hear? Is that why you are getting my money? Who saw him and where did he go?'

'I regret, Excellency – Allah be praised, from what I hear he did no killing, but it is my belief that he was here.'

Hasman sat back in his chair and folded his hands over his belly. This was not the first time Saadi had brought him news of Abu being in the town, but this information followed so closely on the substantiated reports of Abu Hafidh's activities against the Russians – and Colonel Dimarco last night.

It must mean that Abu Hafidh was gaining in confidence – and that he had acquired some means of transport to cover all that ground in one night. The Russian vehicle.

So now Abu Hafidh felt himself at liberty to come and go in the town as he pleased.

'What are they saying about Richard Ahmin?'

'Very little, Excellency. It is known that you have made the house into a fort, they know about the gun on the roof and the lights. They are saying that will not stop Abu Hafidh when he decides to come.'

'They are making this bandit into a hero,' said Hasman.

'They are fools,' agreed Saadi.

'One night he will come,' said Hasman.

'It is expected, Excellency. There are gamblers who put their money on Hafidh, so I have heard.'

Hasman's lips parted slightly. It might

almost have been a smile.

'He will come, but he will not leave. That is sure.'

'It is as Allah wills,' said Saadi piously.

'Allah and the machine-gun,' said Hasman.

Saadi smiled. A joke was a rare thing with Hasman Abdullah Ahmin.

'Excellency,' said Saadi, 'the Colonel has been visiting Richard Ahmin's lady in the hotel, they were privately in her rooms, and they had the whisky drink brought up to them, two bottles. It is being said the Colonel wishes to sleep with her.'

'The Colonel wishes to sleep with many women,' said Hasman. 'He is that kind of man, and it does me no harm.'

'It could be arranged for Richard Ahmin to know about it,' said Saadi. 'Would that meet with Your Excellency's wishes?'

'I am indifferent,' said Hasman. 'It is a matter of no moment. Why do you bring it to me? The woman is nothing. Let Dimarco pleasure himself with her if he chooses. He will still do what I require of him.'

'Assuredly,' said Saadi. 'Excellency, I am indebted to you for many favours, I live but to serve Your Excellency–'

'–You want something,' said Hasman.

'What is it? You had your money last week and you have done little since then to earn more.'

'I am in your debt all the days I live,' said Saadi. 'I pray for nothing but Your Excellency's health and prosperity–'

'–Tell me quickly now,' said Hasman. 'I am busy and I have given you enough of my time.'

'It concerns the Colonel. He has taken one of my women.'

'You have others,' said Hasman. 'You talk too much about Colonel Dimarco. He would not like it.'

'I live under Your Excellency's protection. You are my father and my mother.' Saadi's voice was humble and sad. 'The Colonel has taken Elvira, the most beautiful of my dancers. I am a poor man, Excellency, and Elvira was good for my business. Now patrons ask for her and she is not to be seen, and I lose trade.'

'The Colonel will return her when he is tired of her. This is foolish,' said Hasman. 'You are not expecting him to pay money for your woman?'

'It would be sufficient reward if my humble establishment received fewer inspections from the officials – the police come so often they are frightening my trade away. Your Excellency has but to mention the difficulty to the Colonel. I run an honest business, and I am always happy to co-operate with the police–'

'–You gabble like a market woman,' said Hasman. 'You wish for privileges not granted to your fellow-traders.'

'I can serve Your Excellency better if the Colonel or his men are not chasing my trade away. We are ordered to close too early to be useful – it is later at night when they have been drinking that I am able to hear the things I bring to Your Excellency.'

'I will speak to Colonel Dimarco. Orders will be given.'

'I am your servant for ever, Excellency, and Elvira will continue to fill the Colonel's nights with happiness.'

'You will find out more about Abu Hafidh,' said Hasman. 'I have money for the man who brings me information, true information. If Hafidh comes here at night it is for a purpose, and I wish to know what that is. He is meeting somebody. Find out who. Now go.'

Saadi backed out of the room. It had been a satisfactory meeting. Perhaps that pig of a Colonel would not come swaggering into

The Oasis so often, with his uniform and his men with their guns, ruining trade and paying for nothing ... and taking off his best girls. Saadi padded through the shadows behind the Residence. Hafidh would come again, and he would be bolder – he was a young man of spirit, and people were talking of him because of what he had done the night before.

To make the Colonel look foolish with his men and their guns – to hold them up in the hills all night, and to lose none of his own men ... that had surely been something to smile at.

But Hafidh would come again, and he would make a little mistake, some little mistake because he was young and confident, then Saadi would collect that money Hasman Abdullah Ahmin had ready.

The hotel manager in person brought her the message. Colonel Dimarco was down in the vestibule, he wished to talk with Miss Louise Vannier, and he requested permission to come up and visit her.

'He is being very correct,' the manager whispered. 'It is strange for him. I do not understand it–'

'Show him up,' said Louise. 'At least it's an

improvement on his last visit, but I'd be obliged if you would remain handy, just in case.'

The manager nodded and withdrew. A few moments later there was a tap on the door, and the Colonel entered, once again not in uniform. Sleek and newly shaved, he gave her a nod and said, 'My car is outside. Do you wish to see Richard Ahmin? I am ready to take you to him.'

'I didn't think you meant it,' she said.

'I will wait downstairs,' he said. 'Five minutes. No longer.'

He glanced around the room. 'The bottle of whisky,' he said. 'I do not see it.'

'It's in the sideboard.' She wanted to laugh, the question had been so unexpected, so trivial.

'Wrap it and bring it with you,' he said.

'Colonel,' she said, 'are you serious?'

'Five minutes,' he said. 'No longer.' He went out.

She wasted a few moments, unable to believe it had happened. She had just spent the dreariest day she could remember since she had come to the place, and she had been looking forward to an even more depressing night: Abu couldn't possibly come again so soon.

She found the unopened bottle of whisky and some paper. She darted into her bedroom and made some frantic attempts to coax her hair into obedience, and then her face. She looked like a zombie, she thought. All eyes. How ghastly for Richard. Poor darling.

At the last minute she remembered the case in the wardrobe, and without pausing to question just why she was doing it, she took the little gun and the packet of bullets and stuffed them down into her handbag. Then with the wrapped bottle under her arm she went down.

The vestibule was deserted, except for Colonel Dimarco and the manager hovering hopefully nearby. Without a word the Colonel took the bottle from her and led the way out to where his car waited, a black Mercedes. He normally had an official driver. This time he drove himself, with her on the front seat beside him.

It was only a short ride, at a speed that shifted everything out of the way, and there was no light chat. Dimarco's heavy face was serious and brooding, and he might have been alone in the car.

Louise had been expecting something rather different. He hadn't really looked at her. When they were nearing the gates he hooted, loud and stridently, and a uniformed guard appeared and began to unlock the gates and pull them open.

The Mercedes surged in and stopped by the front door, and Louise noted the men in the garden, sentries with guns that gleamed in the light from the windows. She had heard about the gun on the roof and the lights, everybody in the hotel seemed to know what had been done, and the news had only served to depress her even further. As she got out of the car she could see nothing, and there were no extra lights on. Just the armed men patrolling the grounds.

Before he took her inside, Dimarco said, 'I am keeping my promise. Satisfied?'

'Thank you,' she said.

'I will leave you alone with him,' he said. 'You still don't trust me, do you? You figure it's some kind of a trick, right?'

'I just don't know,' she said simply. 'Does he know I'm coming?'

'He knows nothing. I'm doing you both a favour and don't you forget it.'

He handed her the bottle and took her inside the house. He opened the door into the sitting-room, where Richard Ahmin sat reading quietly, his back to them.

'You got company,' said Dimarco.

Richard turned, saw her and dropped his book. 'Good God,' he whispered. 'Louise, my darling girl – I never thought…'

'Fifteen minutes,' said Dimarco. 'That's your limit.' He stepped aside and closed the door.

They waited, staring at each other. Then he moved and she was in his arms.

'Darling,' she murmured, easing herself free so that she could put the bottle down. But she couldn't escape his mouth nor did she wish to, and there was no need for any words, just the whispered incoherence and the gladness beyond words that took them together down on to the settee. And the minutes ticked along.

Presently she reached down for the handbag she had dropped on the floor. She took out the gun and the packet of ammunition.

'Hide them somewhere, darling,' she said quickly. 'He doesn't know I brought them.'

Richard smiled. 'You're a marvellous girl, did I ever tell you that? A perfectly wonderful and marvellous girl … but I don't need that–'

She put a hand over his mouth, slipped the gun and the ammunition under a cushion. 'You must have something,' she said. 'I'll feel better now I know you're not altogether without something–'

He folded her again in his arms. 'How in the world did you arrange this? It's a beautiful surprise – but how?'

'Dimarco,' she said. 'He offered, the other day. I didn't think he meant it. Then he turned up at the hotel tonight and here I am – I didn't even get time to change my dress.'

'That Dimarco,' said Richard thoughtfully. 'He's tricky – we mustn't trust him too far, darling.'

'I don't,' she said. 'But I'm here, and he made it possible. Now let me look at you. How are you standing all this business, my darling? Just let me look at you.'

'I'm fine,' he said. 'I'm getting fat. You look just wonderful – they're not giving you a bad time are they?'

Lowering her voice, she said, 'Abu came last night – you got my note?'

'I did. Darling, I wish you'd change your mind and clear out of here for a while. I'd feel a lot easier if I knew you were away.'

'And how do you think I'd feel?' she said.

He pointed to the ceiling. 'You've heard what they've done up there? A machine-gun?'

'The whole town knows,' she said.

'Abu mustn't try anything here,' he said.

'I brought you some whisky,' she said. 'It was Dimarco's idea.'

He unwrapped the bottle, smiling, 'A pretty thought,' he said. 'There'll be a price tag, nothing comes free from Tony Dimarco.'

'I don't trust him,' she said. 'Everything about him makes me uneasy. If I had any choice I wouldn't want to have anything to do with him.'

'He's a rogue,' said Richard. 'Listen to this – when I last saw him in here we had a conversation of sorts, and I got the impression that he was open to an offer. It was pretty obvious. We fenced around for a bit, then we got down to the meat of it – for ten thousand American dollars I could consider him on my private side. I could even expect to be liberated quite soon. I haven't seen him since.'

'But what about all the extra defences they've been putting up?' Louise said. 'I think he's changed his mind.'

'I'm puzzled myself,' said Richard. 'He must think I'm a fool.'

'He's an absolute brigand,' she said.

Richard nodded. 'He's in it for the money. He doesn't really give a dam for Hasman except as the current source of his cash. He's a mercenary, and he knows he can't hope to continue here indefinitely. If and when things settle down here there won't be any room for Dimarco and his mob, so he's grabbing all he can while he can. If he sees a better chance somewhere else he'll be off … a pity we have to waste our few minutes together talking about a thug like Dimarco. I'm glad Abu got around to calling on you. He's got all the nerve in the world, from what I heard Hasman has a fit at the very mention of his name.'

'I can believe that,' she said. 'He certainly impressed me, but do you really think he can do anything, Richard? They've made this place into a little fort, there are armed men wherever you look – even Abu can't hope to do anything here now. It would be suicide.'

'Abu will know what they've done. He won't try anything stupid.'

'So what do you think will happen?' she asked.

'I think the Russians are putting extra pressure on Hasman. They've had some casualties, and they won't like that. They've been having an easy ride here so far, and I gather they haven't been exactly happy about Tony Dimarco and his operations. The more internal squabbling there is the better I for one will like it. Hasman might even be persuaded to give them the boot, although I don't think that's very likely just yet. So I intend to sit tight and let things simmer a little longer ... but I do wish you'd be sensible and get out of here.'

'No,' she said flatly.

'You worry me.' His voice was gentle. He stroked her cheek. She caught his hand and kissed it.

'You can't send me away,' she murmured.

The door opened and Dimarco came in briskly. He gave the two of them a sharp glance.

'Sorry,' he said. 'I gotta blow the whistle on you now.'

Richard stood up. 'You've been most kind, Colonel,' he said. 'We appreciate it.'

'That's me,' said Tony. 'The sunshine kid. Everything okay with you now?'

'Quite,' said Richard. 'But there's one little matter that bothers me. The last time we met we had a conversation of a delicate nature – I hope it hasn't slipped your mind?'

'You gotta be kidding,' said Tony. 'So?'

'Perhaps I'm being unduly nervous,' said Richard. 'I note that I am being more

136

strongly guarded than ever. It doesn't quite fit in with what we were talking about. Why all the extra precautions?'

'You never hear of camouflage?' said Tony. 'Looks good, don't it? His Excellency reckons I'm doing a fine job here. It would take an army to spring you now, right? And you don't have any army, right?'

'A fair summary,' said Richard.

Tony grinned at both of them. 'You didn't figure I was gonna loaf around and let this Abu feller come in here and help himself to my prisoner? Hell no, then I'd be the guy with egg on his face. You follow me?'

'So it's all bogus?' said Richard. 'Window-dressing?'

'I never said that. Anybody who shows himself around here at night won't have a prayer, and you can pass the good word along.'

'So just where does that leave me?' said Richard quietly.

'You want out, correct?' said Tony. 'You figure you been in here long enough?'

Richard nodded.

'So listen,' said Tony crisply. 'You write a proper letter to your bank, same as we talked about the other day. You authorize them to transfer a credit of ten thousand

137

good old American dollars right away, to me, Antonio Angelo Dimarco. I got a small account in Tangier, at the *Banque Marocaine du Commerce Extérieur.* You got that?'

'I'm right with you,' said Richard.

'You tell them to rush it,' said Tony. 'Soon as I hear it's okay we're in business together.'

'How do I get the letter out?' asked Richard.

'I'll take it,' said Louise quickly.

'You try to post it here, lady' said Tony, 'and it won't leave the country.'

'I'll take it with me,' she said.

'Then they won't let you back in,' said Tony. 'It will suit old Hasman fine not to have you hanging around here. Once you're out they'll put the bar up. That what you want?'

'So we leave it with you to get it out,' she said.

'Air mail, Casablanca, first thing tomorrow,' said Tony.

Richard went over to the desk. He sat and thought for a moment, then began to write. Tony stood over him and watched.

'I must be getting soft,' he said. 'I'm sticking my neck out for peanuts.'

Richard glanced at him and smiled. 'You quoted a price, Colonel. I accepted it. So stop acting like a bandit.'

Tony grinned, uninsulted.

'If all goes well,' said Richard, 'if the conclusion is satisfactory, I may be inclined to look on this as a down payment. I value my liberty.'

'Don't we all?' Tony took the letter, read through it, and found it what he wanted. He watched Richard address an envelope to a London bank.

'This isn't the quickest way to arrange this,' said Richard. 'You could send it by cable.'

'And have some goddam post office clerk know all about it?' said Tony. 'My name and everything? If this leaks we get the chopper but fast.' He looked across at Louise. 'And you'd better remember that as well. You could do it by phone from outside, sure you could, but you wouldn't get back in.'

She reflected, avoiding Richard's eye.

'You want to stay here,' said Tony. 'So this is the way it'll have to be.'

'It will take time,' said Richard. 'A few days.'

'I'll know soon enough,' said Tony. 'What's it gonna be, lady?'

'I'm staying,' she said. 'I know nothing about it. Do it your way.'

'You stay put and keep your nose clean,' Tony said to Richard.

'We're trusting you, Colonel,' said Richard softly.

'You got no choice,' said Tony. 'If this comes unzipped we're all dead ducks.'

'You haven't told me what you're planning to do,' said Richard. 'I'm buying this sight unseen.'

'Like you said, you gotta trust me.' Tony patted his pocket. 'This little letter is dynamite. Think I don't know that?'

'Suppose it doesn't work?' said Richard.

'You better pray it does. Let's go, lady.'

'One moment,' said Richard. 'I hear your reputation has become a little tarnished of late, Colonel. Take it from me, Hasman shouldn't be relied on too far, and you are only an emergency measure.'

'Let me worry about that,' said Tony. 'I'm tricky myself.' He poked Richard in the chest with a finger. 'You do your own sweating. I'll let you know when you can expect some action, but if this thing looks like getting fouled up I won't wait around for the funeral.'

'Very comforting' said Richard.

'I got my ear to the ground,' said Tony.

'I sincerely hope so,' said Richard. He

slipped his hand under Louise's arm and walked her over to the door. He could feel how tense she was. He made her look at him, and tried to make her smile.

But Tony Dimarco was hovering there. An alien presence. Watching.

'Look after yourself, my sweet,' Richard said gently. 'Perhaps the Colonel will be kind enough to bring you again.'

'Don't bet on it,' said Tony. 'We been in here long enough. You all ready, lady?'

He held her arm and she had to go with him.

EIGHT

He put her in the car, and as he got in beside her he said, 'You chat about this visit in the wrong place and you put the skids under all of us, you got me?'

'Why should I talk? It's obviously irregular. But you got what you were after, the chance to pick up some extra money.'

'Is that bad?' he said. 'You get your money easy, I have to sweat, that makes me some kind of a rat?'

He started the engine and let the car roll slowly down to the gates. He flashed his lights and the gates were opened. They surged out.

'Hasman will know about this, won't he?' she said. 'You can't hope to keep it a secret, all those soldiers have seen us...'

'I'll tell him myself,' said Tony. 'Tonight. He'll think I've been smart, dangling the bait in front of the prisoner, letting him see what he's missing. I won't tell him I left you alone with him. He'll figure the same as I do – we got your boy friend worried a bit more.'

'That's pretty crude,' she said. 'Using me like that.'

Tony laughed. 'We're crude folk around here, hadn't you noticed?'

'I noticed,' she said. 'You're garbage, Colonel Dimarco.'

'I been using my head,' he said. 'Old Hasman will get the point, anything that helps to upset Richard Ahmin is okay with Hasman, soften him up, know what I mean?'

'You make me wish I hadn't agreed to come with you,' she said.

'You're a good looking dame,' said Tony. 'I bet you got Richard going back there.'

'Shut up,' she said. 'You nauseate me.'

'You look real good when you're riled,' he said.

'I don't want to hear any more from you,' she said.

'I did you both a favour – wasn't it worth it?'

'You did it for money,' she said. 'I think you'd do anything for money, but you're really rather a stupid man. You're two clumsy and obvious. I don't think for one minute that you will be able to deceive Hasman much longer. He isn't a complete fool.'

'This letter I got in my pocket,' said Tony. 'It might just go astray. Suppose I decide not to have it sent? Suppose I show it to Hasman, wouldn't that prove to him what a loyal kind of feller I am? That would rate a bonus for me, don't you figure it that way?'

She glanced at him quickly. His face was quite serious. And she knew he wasn't just talking for effect. This was the real Tony Dimarco, with the instincts of a louse.

'Just give it some thought, lady,' he said. 'You figure me for a bastard, so maybe I'll behave like one, if I have to.'

'If you'll stop the car I'd rather walk the rest of the way,' she said.

He put on speed and there was nothing she could do but sit there beside him. When they reached the hotel he followed her in and across the vestibule and up the stairs, and he was right there behind her when she opened the door of her apartment.

She wasn't quick enough to shut him out. He followed her in and shut the door.

She rounded on him. 'We've had this stupid scene before,' she said wearily. 'I've had my fill of you for one evening. Just go away – or do I have to make another fuss?'

'Nobody will come,' he said. 'No good using that phone, no good shouting.' He turned the key in the lock and took the key out and bounced it on his hand.

'You're being as stupid as I thought,' she said. 'There must be plenty of women here who would welcome your company, I'm not one of them, can't you get that through your thick skull? You don't interest me in the slightest–'

He reached her in a couple of strides. His left arm snaked around her, holding her tight and pining her arms to her sides. With his right hand he tilted her face up to him. His grip was so strong and so sudden that her feet barely touched the floor.

'Now you listen, baby,' he said, 'I don't aim to take any more of that crap from you. Enough is enough, okay? I never raped a woman yet, but there's that bed in there and I'm getting good and tired of your yapping, so just watch it. You want me to give your boy friend a fair shake so you better mind your step.'

He released her. She dropped into a chair and massaged her arms, not looking at him, and she was more frightened than she would admit to herself. She was quite at his mercy, and she had been so sure she could handle him.

Tony lit a cigar, watching her. He reckoned he was half way there and it wouldn't be any rape. She might be an educated lady,

145

used to nice manners and being made a fuss of … but she'd be like all the rest of them once he got her far enough along.

'I didn't mean to hurt you,' he said. 'You hear me?'

'Think nothing of it,' she said. 'I shouldn't have expected anything else, but you don't have to prove to me that you are a male animal, Colonel Dimarco. Now suppose we just agree to end this little social encounter.'

'I got a better idea,' said Tony. 'You freshen yourself up and I'll take you out for some food, kind of get better acquainted, after all, we got plenty in common.'

She sat and looked at him. Dinner with Tony Dimarco was quite the last thing she had in mind.

'No strings, Colonel?' she said. 'I'm in no mood for another wrestling bout.'

'I know how to treat a lady,' he said. 'You just shouldn't be so goddam beautiful. I'll be downstairs in the bar.'

He nodded at her, went over and unlocked the door. 'I'll show you places here you never seen before. Be educational, know what I mean?'

'I expect I do,' she said.

'No strings,' he said, and let himself out.

He took her to the *Tour Hassan,* an impressive white villa set back off the main boulevard. In quieter times it had functioned as a town club for rich landlords. In addition to the restaurant there were gaming rooms, ornamental gardens with fountains, and private facilities for more intimate entertainments.

Louise had heard about it and thought she knew what to expect. The dining-room was largely empty, and the Colonel was obviously a favoured client. They received excellent and obsequious attention, and the food was considerably better than Louise had been eating at her hotel, in spite of the hotel's exorbitant prices.

Tony was a hearty eater and saw no reason to be ashamed of it or apologetic. It was good chow and he had a beautiful girl sitting opposite him, so everything was going okay. When he had time he talked some of the usual stuff at her, and he thought she seemed interested. She looked real cool. Class, you couldn't miss it.

That letter he had in his pocket, she would be remembering that. It sort of tied them together and she couldn't pretend he didn't count, because she couldn't do without him. Hell, they were on the same side.

Right? Tony felt good and expansive.

They took coffee in the inside courtyard where the fountains danced in the soft lights. There was distant music and the scent of flowers. Romantic.

'You like a crack at the tables?' said Tony. 'They run baccarat, roulette–'

'No thank you,' she said. 'Gambling isn't my thing at all, but don't let me stop you, Colonel. I'll be quite happy watching you losing your money.'

Tony grinned at her through the smoke of his cigar. 'Forget it,' he said. 'It's all rigged anyway. I just thought it might amuse you.'

'I'm having a lovely evening.' Her voice was nicely polite. 'This is a pleasant place, but it doesn't seem to be too well patron-ized.'

'Like this most nights,' said Tony. 'Used to be a real money-spinner, but the heavy spenders stay home nights, and the rich tourists don't find their way up here.'

'Ahminad doesn't exactly invite visitors,' she said.

'Take it up with Hasman. He's the boss.'

'You don't feel you have a certain responsibility yourself?' she said pleasantly. 'Your methods are pretty brutal, Colonel. You are hardly an apostle of peace.'

'I keep them in line,' said Tony. 'I have to see Hasman isn't around when the shooting starts. So long as I keep him from being spread over the sidewalk I'll be okay.'

'And where does Richard Ahmin fit in?' she said quietly.

'Insurance,' said Tony. 'If it hadn't been for me Hasman would have tossed him into the jail. That's what the Commies want. You might say I'm playing both ends against the middle.'

She watched him thoughtfully. 'When will you decide to do something for Richard?'

'When it's the right time.'

'And when will that be?'

'Maybe sooner than you think,' he said.

'Colonel,' she said, 'be honest with me – is this all just an elaborate game you're playing with us? Do you really intend to help Richard to get away?'

'You think I'm a louse. You think I'm giving you the dirty end of the stick. For ten thousand dollars. Correct?'

Without waiting for her to answer he stubbed his cigar out with a sudden spurt of violence that surprised her. He dug into his pocket and took out the envelope. He slapped it on the table between them and flicked it contemptuously so that it skidded

149

into her lap.

'Okay,' he said, 'have it your way. Tear that up. Burn it – hell, what should I care? Listen, I'll liberate that feller of yours when the right time comes, and I won't take a goddam cent from any of you. I'll give him to you as a present, lady – that's the kind of a bastard I am.'

She had to meet his vicious look, all the open hostility in his eyes, and she felt herself blushing. She fumbled with the envelope and pushed it back to him.

'I apologize,' she said quietly. 'I was all wrong–'

'Good,' he said. 'So long as we understand each other.'

'We do,' she said. 'I'm sorry.'

'That's okay.' He slid the envelope back into his pocket. That had been a smart play, he thought. It had fooled her all the way. 'The plain fact is that you don't trust me,' he said.

'It's a difficult situation,' she said mildly.

'There's always an angle,' said Tony. 'I have to figure out which is the right one. We want to keep Richard Ahmin all in one piece, right?'

'Right,' she said steadily. 'Nothing else matters to me, Colonel.'

150

He was going to make the obvious remark that Richard Ahmin was a lucky guy, but from the tone of her voice and the way she was looking at him he didn't think she was in the mood for any sweet talking.

'I'm nervous and I'm worried,' she said. 'I can't pretend I'm not. I want Richard out of here, and there isn't much I wouldn't do to make that happen.'

She wasn't just talking, Tony was sure of that. She had plenty of nerve.

'Let's move along,' he said. 'How about hitting one of the dives where they have native dancing? You ever seen any?'

'Not yet,' she said. 'I thought they had all been closed up?'

'We let one or two of them still operate. It might be good for a laugh. Nothing too raw, understand?'

She smiled. 'Strictly educational?'

'In a manner of speaking,' said Tony, and grinned at her.

As they left she noticed that there seemed to be no question of any bill being presented, nor did Tony appear to expect one. So she guessed it wasn't part of his habit to pay for anything anywhere. He would see nothing wrong in that.

Saadi was in his office when he heard the Colonel Dimarco and a blonde lady were arriving. He hurried out and welcomed them to his humble establishment, conducted them to a table with the best view of the floor show which was about to take place, and assured the Colonel that he had some French champagne of a superlative quality with the compliments of the house for the Colonel and his lady.

Tony slapped him on the back. 'This guy's the biggest rogue in town. That right, Saadi boy?'

Saadi smiled his obsequious sideways smile. The Colonel was always a great gentleman for the jokes. Very funny gentleman. He hustled off to fetch the champagne himself.

Now this was surely of interest: Dimarco out for a social evening with Richard Ahmin's woman. Soon they would be sleeping together, if they had not done so already. Richard Ahmin would not like that.

He darted into the little dungeon that served as a dressing-room and warned the performers to clean their acts just a little because they had some distinguished visitors who must not be offended too much. He posted his sharpest waiter on the

Colonel's table to pick up their conversation, and he was remembering with no pleasure that the last time Dimarco had been on his premises it had cost him the services of Elvira.

Before the lights dimmed for the floor show he took some snaps of the Colonel and the woman from the observation hole in his office overlooking the floor. They were smiling together and the champagne was on the table. Somehow he would contrive to have a few prints dropped where Richard Ahmin would see them. They would show him how his woman spent her evenings.

Abu Hafidh and Burabin waited silently in the shadows. They were watching the high wall and the gates of the armoury where the sentry stood. It was after eleven and the duty officer from the barracks next door had just made his rounds. Now he would be back in the mess, and he wouldn't be visible again until reveille. The junior officers took their night duties lightly. Why make life uncomfortable when the senior officers didn't give a damn?

The sentry did a little stamping up and down. There was nobody about to be impressed at his soldierly bearing, so he presently retired to his box and took time off for a smoke.

They saw the flare of the match, and they started. They appeared on each side of the sentry box. Burabin took the rifle the sentry had placed between his knees, and Abu had a knife at his throat before the sentry really knew he was no longer alone.

'You will be silent, friend,' said Abu softly. 'Agreed? Unless you wish to die now?'

The sentry made the only choice. They pulled him inside the gates and held him hard against the wall, facing in. Burabin clubbed him with the rifle and caught his body and let it fall quietly.

The buildings all around them were dark, except for the one where the duty guard should be – a Corporal and one other soldier.

They stole across and Abu peeped into the lighted window. There were two bunks, one of them occupied by a man in his vest and pants; very dark and muscular and hairy; he was reading a magazine, and from a peg in the wall hung a tunic with chevrons; there was no sign of the other one who should be there.

Abu and Burabin withdrew into the shelter of a truck.

They could deal with the Corporal, they could get the keys and kept themselves to what they had come for. The missing soldier was the difficulty. He might return at the wrong time. He might see the unconscious body of his comrade by that wall over there. If they waited too long Mossou would arrive with the jeep before they were ready, and that would not be good.

They could hear the barracks noises from over the wall. Canned music. Men's voices, shouting, singing after a fashion.

The Corporal came to the door a few yards from where they squatted. He cupped his hands to his mouth and shouted: '*Balek, balek – Tizi-ben-Zalagh* ... attention, Tizi you son of a goat...!'

It was a memorable shout and soon footsteps sounded over the gravel and a soldier appeared at a trot, carrying a pot of coffee, and the two soldiers went inside, the Corporal's voice still rumbling.

They were drinking their coffee when the invasion took place and this time there was no time for any challenge. The Corporal had his back to the door. Burabin pinned him from the rear with one arm around his throat, pressing on his windpipe and spilling the hot coffee down his all but naked chest, which was the least of his misfortunes, because Burabin kicked his legs from under him and slammed him to the floor, and then hit him behind the ear with a short piece of iron – a neat and largely silent victory.

The survivor was not too sharp in his wits. He was young and not big enough, and lacked the offensive spirit. He dithered when he just might have run for salvation. But then he had seen his Corporal dealt with so ignominiously, and the Corporal was reputed to be one of the hardest men in the unit.

He dropped his mug of coffee, opened his mouth but found himself too scared to scream as Abu advanced on him. He retreated into the corner by the bunks and he would have been very happy to burrow his way out through the wall.

Abu was by instinct no fist fighter. Normally he would use a knife or a gun. Now he used neither. The soldier made a crazy dart for the door. Abu tripped him and kicked him in the head as he fell, then again more carefully under the jaw. It was more than enough.

Burabin had already lifted the keys off the board on the wall, the keys to the rooms along the corridor. This was the point of the expedition and they would have to be quick to keep to their timing. They had to risk putting the lights on in order to select what they had come for.

They had to make three hurried trips, carrying the loads between them out to the gates, and the sentry they had immobilized was beginning to make moaning noises, but he was in no state to interfere yet. But they hurried.

They heard Mossou arrive outside, no lights showing, right on schedule. He helped to load what they had brought out – some of the new automatic carbines with ammunition, and a case of the recently delivered CS gas grenades.

With the cargo they had on the jeep there was going to be no room for Burabin, that had been agreed, but he had a safe place to stay for the night.

He slapped the bonnet of the jeep, it might have been a horse, and cheerfully whispered it was time for them to go. Without waiting for them to drive off he turned and ran quickly back.

'Wait,' murmured Abu. 'That Burabin, he looks for more trouble – he takes too many risks, that one…'

'All has gone well with you?' whispered Mossou.

'So far,' said Abu. 'But Burabin has not gone back there to say any prayers, I think.'

The heard the first detonation inside the building, sharp and crisp – a grenade, clearly; then another very quickly after, followed by a series of smaller explosions that built rapidly into a crescendo, irregular, without any pattern. Then the barred window high up in the wall burst open, shattering glass into the road in front of them. Spurts of flames like waving fingers licked out into the air and dark curls of smoke lifted, lit underneath by the fires.

And they knew why Burabin had gone back and it had little to do with prayer, as Abu had surmised. He must have found some fused grenades, and he had tossed them in among the ammunition.

They waited, their engine running. Burabin appeared, sprinting like a youth, which he was not. There was joy on his sardonic face. He waved both hands at them, dismissing them urgently. He bolted across the road, and vanished in the shadows. Nobody was going to trace him. Ammunition was still exploding, and the fire had now taken a good hold.

Mossou sent the jeep surging round the nearest corner. They could hear the shouting from the barracks, but there were no dangerous witnesses abroad on the road yet. Sensible citizens who lived nearby kept themselves at home, because they knew too well that shooting at night in the town was no matter for any civilians to show too much interest in – one might get oneself arrested just for being found too near the scene of the incident too soon.

This surely sounded like some kind of a battle near the barracks, and soldiers were paid to fight battles. Later when it was all quiet it would be safe to venture out and seek information. But not yet, it would be much too dangerous.

Mossou jockeyed the jeep through a maze of unfrequented lanes at a moderate speed, and at no time did they appear on any street where the lights might give them away; there were very few jeeps in the town, and they didn't intend to get stuck in any traffic tangle where some inquisitive stranger might notice the unusual load on their back seat.

They threaded a tortuous way through the older part of the town. Past the *souk* where some interest had already been aroused, and little excited groups of loungers were making noisy guesses as to the nature of the catastrophe. Out through the old gateway that once had been closed at nightfall when the town had been a walled enclosure.

The jeep bucked and skidded as they crossed the ancient caravan camping site outside the walls; now there were mostly truck and lorries in place of camels, petrol cans and untidy piles of old tyres.

Heading north, they stopped on the high ground and looked back. They could see the fire above the muddle of roofs. With all that ammunition exploding still no fire-fighting party would risk entering the building, so there was a reasonable chance that the fire would spread to the barracks next door.

Abu Hafidh and Mossou exchanged satisfied glances.

'That Burabin has my respect,' said Mossou.

'A memorable evening,' said Abu, and they drove on.

NINE

The floor show had been extravagantly announced, but it was proving something of a disappointment, certainly to Colonel Dimarco.

In the enforced absence of the talented Elvira, the starring role was being performed by a plumpish belly-dancer named Lalla, who was being obviously handicapped by having to wear a *cache-sexe*, to which she was not accustomed. It would not remain in its discreet place when Lalla really got busy on her gyrations, and ribald comments were being offered by some of the clients who knew what Lalla really looked like, and who saw no point in her comic modesty.

The supporting chorus of dancers were poorly drilled, locally recruited, and of minimal talent, poor things. They tried, bare-breasted, powdered and still shining with sweat in the close atmosphere and smoke. Bobbing and kicking, with their fixed smiles.

161

Tony Dimarco leaned across to Louise. 'Had enough?'

'Please,' she said thankfully. She had been going over in her mind what she would say to him when they got back to the hotel, because on no account was he going to come up to her apartment, which was certainly what he expected to do. That was what this evening outing was all in aid of, she was sure of that.

A comedian had bounced out into the spot light, and he had already launched into his patter in quick-fire Arabic that she couldn't follow, but it was evidently dirty enough for most of his audience.

Saadi had appeared behind the Colonel's chair, and in a highly secretive fashion began to give him the news that had just reached him, and as he listened Dimarco began to grin because this was a recital that he enjoyed since his outfit had not been involved.

'Excuse me,' he said to Louise, getting to his feet. 'Just as well we're leaving, I have to break off anyway. There's been some shooting at the barracks and I'll have to be around. Okay?'

Saadi escorted them out and expressed the hope that his establishment would again be so honoured, and so forth.

As they drove back to the hotel they caught glimpses of the fire, and now there were plenty of excited citizens abroad.

'You don't seem very worried,' said Louise. 'What's been happening?'

'Some kind of a raid,' said Tony, 'and not a bad job at that. Not my guys this time, the army boys caught it, so I'm not crying too much. They knocked out the guards at the armoury and lifted some of the iron-mongery, guns and stuff. Then they set fire to the place and beat it. That's what I hear so far.'

'Do they know who did it?' she asked.

Tony glanced across at her. 'Are you fooling with me? Abu Hafidh pulled it, who else? He sure gets about, and now he's got some extra hardware, and that's not so good. Hasman will blow his stack over this.'

They drew up at the hotel. He helped her out. 'See you soon,' he said and got back into the car and drove off.

Colonel Marhaba, the Army Commander, was a tall, sad man who had always found his duties just a little too much for him. He had few of the attributes of a successful soldier, but he was well-connected himself,

163

and his wife was the daughter of one of Hasman's oldest supporters. He had, naturally, never seen any active service, but he had inherited an excellent seat on a horse, and could look an impressively martial figure on the parade ground so long as his adjutant was handy to tell him what he ought to be doing.

He had, of course, not welcomed the arrival of Dimarco and his gang of ruffians, but he had been far too tactful to raise any objections with His Excellency since that might draw attention to his own inadequacies. As far as possible he avoided having any contact with Tony, and since he seldom took any overt action that was not too difficult.

So he was not too pleased when he saw Dimarco thrusting his way authoritatively through the crowd at the scene of the fire.

The armoury was a blackened and gutted shell; all the live ammunition had been exploded, and the main barrack block next door had been badly damaged so that most of the troops had been evacuated. It was thus an area where confusion reigned, in no small measure. And Colonel Marhaba's sad face was sadder than ever.

'Hi, Colonel,' said Tony breezily, 'you took

164

quite a beating there, like any help?'

'It is nothing.' Marhaba's voice was frosty.

'Coulda fooled me,' said Tony. 'Looks like you just lost your armoury and most of your barracks.'

'We have it under control.' Clearly Colonel Marhaba wished to terminate the interview.

'I'd call it a mess if it happened to me,' said Tony. 'They hit you with your pants down, right?'

Marhaba shrugged. Some of his junior officers were listening to the conversation, and enjoying it, from the smiles on their faces.

'It was a cowardly outrage,' said Marhaba in statesmanlike tones. 'It will not go unpunished.'

'So you got the guys who did it?'

They both knew it was not a serious question.

'Too bad,' said Tony. 'They got a nerve.'

'Brigands,' said Marhaba with feeling and staring right at Tony Dimarco. 'Bandits, the riffraff from the hills, they will not dare to do this again.'

'Wouldn't be any point, would it?' said Tony amiably. 'I hear they got what they wanted.'

'I have duties to attend to.' Marhaba turned smartly and marched off. It had just come into his mind that he should be preparing a court-martial to deal with those three uniformed peasants who were responsible for this disgrace. His Excellency would expect no less. There was also the report he had yet to make in person to His Excellency. He did not look forward to that – the less one had to do directly with Hasman the quieter life was, especially in recent weeks and since the arrival of that insolent and ill-mannered Dimarco. Colonel indeed! It was an insult to the military profession.

When Marhaba presented himself to report to Hasman Abdullah Ahmin, he was disconcerted to find Tony Dimarco already there and looking pleased with himself. When Marhaba intimated that he would prefer to make his report as Commander of the Army in private, Hasman told him not to be a fool.

'Colonel Dimarco is in my confidence,' said Hasman. 'I have reason to value his advice. Continue.'

Marhaba repeated the embroidered version he had listened to from the Corporal and the two unlucky soldiers who were now all three under close arrest. It had been a full-scale assault by at least a score of armed men, probably more.

'I have convened a court-martial for tomorrow,' said Marhaba importantly.

A stuffed shirt, thought Tony Dimarco, playing at soldiers.

'My men were outnumbered,' said Marhaba, 'and it was a treacherous attack, but discipline must be maintained. You agree, Excellency?'

Hasman glanced at Tony.

'You sure you got the right version, Colonel?' said Tony. 'After you left me down there because you didn't want to talk to me any more, when you thought I was sticking my nose in, remember? Well, I talked with some of your men, guys who were first on the scene after it happened–'

'–That was most improper of you,' said Marhaba. 'That was not in accordance with military etiquette, Dimarco. Even you should know that much.'

'Do not interrupt, Colonel Marhaba,' said Hasman sharply. 'This is a serious matter. So listen.'

'I talked to the guys who saw the sentry,' said Tony. 'He said he was jumped by two men, just two, Colonel.'

'That is not possible,' said Marhaba, but his voice lacked conviction.

'That's the way it was,' said Tony. 'They knocked him out but he was coming round when they were leaving and he says there was only one car and it wasn't a big one. He admits he saw the guy who did all the damage in the armoury, but he was too scared to try anything – I reckon he showed good sense there. It was a small raiding party and they knew what they were after.'

Marhaba stared at Tony Dimarco malevolently. 'That is not the information I received.'

'They fooled you,' said Tony. 'They made it look better for themselves, so they gave you a yarn and you swallowed it.'

'Dimarco, I find your manner offensive,' said Marhaba stiffly.

'Colonel Dimarco,' said Tony pleasantly. 'You don't outrank me, buddie.'

'That is enough,' snapped Hasman. 'We have all been made to look foolish. Colonel Marhaba, what was taken from your armoury? Do you know that?'

'It is difficult to estimate,' said Marhaba. 'There has been much damage done. I fear there is little left of the small-arms, and most of the live ammunition has been exploded.'

'Very good,' said Hasman acidly. 'So we have the pretence of an armed force with no guns and no ammunition. Have I put it correctly? We are in fact without means of defence?'

Marhaba shuffled about unhappily. 'It may be a little better than that, Excellency.'

'I sincerely hope so,' said Hasman. 'Continue.'

'There will be items we can salvage. I will detail a party to work on it in the morning.'

'You better hope you don't get hit again tonight,' said Tony with a huge grin.

'That is hardly possible,' said Marhaba.

'Don't bet on it,' said Tony. 'That was Abu Hafidh who called on you tonight. It sticks out a mile. Your sentry described him, Colonel buddie. That Abu could steal your lot blind and they wouldn't know a goddam thing about until it was all over, same as tonight – bingo!'

'You talk nonsense,' said Marhaba.

'You better double your guards all round,' said Tony. 'Have your guys sleep with their rifles under their beds, if you got any beds left.'

Marhaba found it more dignified to ignore Tony's insulting comments. He addressed himself to Hasman.

'The town is now under control, Excellency. I have patrols out to keep the streets clear. There will be no further disturbance.'

'If there is, Colonel Marhaba,' said Hasman, 'I advise you to take a long furlough, without your uniform, you will not be needing it again. Understood? Before the night is over you will give me a detailed report on the state of your force, how much material you have lost, and you will assist Colonel Dimarco to interrogate those three men of yours. This time I will have the truth.'

'My pleasure,' said Tony Dimarco, getting to his feet. 'Let's go, Colonel.' He led the way out and Marhaba could do nothing but follow.

The Corporal and the two soldiers were under guard in the same cell. They were bruised, but not actually depressed. What had happened to them could happen to anybody, and the Corporal had coached them carefully. They would stick to the same story, and they had the injuries to prove what a gallant resistance they had put up against overwhelming numbers.

The arrival of Tony Dimarco engendered some uneasiness. They knew enough about him and his methods to know he would not be easy to fool, not like their own Colonel.

Tony promptly had them shifted into separate cells, stopped them smoking, and told the guards what would happen to them if they communicated with the prisoners, and he put it with such originality that they had to believe him.

He left the three men to sweat alone for a while and had himself conducted round the area of desolation by a sergeant who knew his job. Colonel Marhaba had closeted himself in his office with his adjutant and some files of ammunition and weapons returns that they both knew were inaccurate and far from complete out of which they hoped to fabricate a report that would satisfy His Excellency. Marhaba had made it clear he had no wish to associate further with that ill-bred Dimarco.

After a suitable interval, Tony returned to the cells, subjected each unfortunate to a long, silent examination, during which he shook his head and paced around the prisoner with a foreboding expression that could mean nothing but disaster ahead. Even the Corporal was sweating. This man was a bastard – standing rigidly at attention until his joints creaked, the Corporal knew that much. All the stories he had heard about Dimarco must be true.

Tony handled them one by one, beginning with the sentry whose memory began rapidly to clear as Tony prodded him neatly and tirelessly. There had been two raiders, and one of them had been Abu Hafidh or Abu Hafidh's double. Before the explosions had begun they had carried cases out of the armoury, and there had been a third man who had driven their vehicle. There had been no shooting, and the sentry admitted that the damage to his own skull had been done with his own rifle.

Tony got it all down in writing, and the sentry sighed. The Corporal tried to come the old soldier for a very little while. He had been attacked from the rear. He had never even seen his assailant. There could have been a dozen of them.

'Your mate in the armoury saw them,' said Tony. 'There were only two. You must have been deaf if you let a dozen guys creep up on you inside. The sentry says two. Think again, Corporal.'

When he left, Tony had signed statements from each of them, indicating that it had been a neat and quick little job – nothing at all to be ashamed of, if you were on the other side of the fence.

It was now nearly three in the morning, but Hasman was still available, and he listened with interest as Tony made his report and handed in the three statements.

'That's about the truth of it,' said Tony. 'At least one case of grenades, those new tear-gas jobs. Maybe ten new rifles and some ammo – two guys carrying the gear out and some kind of a buggy waiting outside the gate. Nice timing. Before they drive off one of them starts the fireworks in the armoury, then they take off real sharp. There'll be plenty of talk around the town after this.'

Hasman tugged his hooked nose between finger and thumb.

'Abu Hafidh?'

'Who else?' said Tony. 'He's got a lot of nerve lately, now he's got that new hardware and I don't like that much. They knew what they wanted and they took it. Those gas jobs could make a lot of grief in a crowded street, and they're dead easy to handle and carry around. We can expect more action, and that comic Colonel isn't gonna be much help.'

'I am giving you full authority to take any measures you think fit,' said Hasman, 'as from now. When Colonel Marhaba finds it convenient to report here I will instruct him accordingly.'

'He'll have a seizure,' said Tony placidly. 'He thinks I'm low-life.'

'That worries you?'

Tony Dimarco smiled. 'Not so's you'd notice. Now we'll need an issue of gas masks, at least for my men looking after Richard Ahmin – that's where I figure Abu will use those grenades, if they toss them inside the grounds at night we'd never know what the hell was going on.'

'A possibility,' said Hasman. 'But we have no masks, have we?'

'I can get some,' said Tony. 'You give me the right piece of official paper, I can do a deal with the Army guys down in Casablanca. As soon as it's light I'll take a truck and go down myself, make sure there's no snarl-up this time. The way things are going around here, I don't trust any of those guys much. You want anything done you gotta do it yourself. I'll be back in town before the morning's over. Okay, Excellency?'

Hasman agreed; he was impressed with Tony's efficiency and speed, in sharp contrast to Colonel Marhaba's sloppiness. And Tony was relieved to have found a reasonable excuse for the trip to Casablanca. He would air-mail the letter, and then wait to see how things looked.

This Abu Hafidh might be more of a handful than he expected. He could louse it up.

'I hear you have been out entertaining Richard Ahmin's woman,' said Hasman.

Tony Dimarco immediately thought of that creep Saadi. He wondered if Hasman had yet heard about the meeting between Louise Vannier and Richard Ahmin. It would reach him eventually, so Tony decided to get in first.

'I took her out for some chow,' he said. 'But that wasn't the whole of it–'

'I wish for no details,' said Hasman quite amiably. 'Your sex exploits are of no interest to me, discreet or indiscreet. If she amuses you I have no objection, as long as it does not interfere with your work here for me.'

'I figured that,' said Tony. 'I took her last night and let her talk to Richard Ahmin, just for a coupla minutes. I was there all the time. Sort of dangled her in front of him and he couldn't do a goddam thing about her, not with me slap there in the middle. It got him all stirred up, like he wanted to give it to her then and there.'

Hasman opened a drawer in his desk, took out a photograph and slid it across to Tony. It showed the two of them sitting together in the friendliest fashion at the table at Saadi's place, Tony leaning to her to pour more wine into her glass, both of them smiling.

'If Richard Ahmin saw that,' said Hasman, 'it might excite him even more.'

'Goddam,' said Tony with just a touch of reverence in his voice. 'He's an operator, that Saadi. He doesn't miss a trick – so what does he reckon this will buy him?'

'He is an opportunist, as you are,' said Hasman. 'He has his uses. I have been thinking – suppose this picture just happened to fall into Richard Ahmin's hands, it might provoke him into trying to escape, which might be unfortunate for him. The woman is important to him, and he will know of your reputation. It cannot make him feel happy to think that you entertain her at night clubs while he remains a prisoner.'

'If one of my guys shoots him while he is trying to escape, nobody will blame you,' said Tony.

'I will deplore it in public,' said Hasman. 'After all, he is of my family – a misguided young man who came under the wrong influence and let himself be used by hot-headed malcontents. Most unfortunate. Then you will be free to devote all of your time and your men to dealing with this bandit, Abu Hafidh. Does that seem to you to be a fair assessment of the situation, Colonel Dimarco?'

'It might work,' said Tony. 'He's a tricky guy, what I've seen of him, but he might fall for it.'

'Try it,' said Hasman. 'If he is the man I think he is, he will surely want to do something. He is simple.'

'I wouldn't say that,' said Tony. 'He's not dumb, he's smart enough.'

'He is a prisoner,' said Hasman. 'She is free to go and do what she pleases. Women are women, and you have an acknowledged appetite for women.'

'That's right,' said Tony complacently. 'I usually get what I want. I haven't made that one yet, but I will.'

Hasman smiled remotely. 'Arrange to have a photographer available. That would solve it.'

Tony grinned as he made for the door. 'Now that wouldn't be nice, would it, Excellency?'

'One small thing,' said Hasman. 'Saadi would like to have his young dancer returned, Elvira – he is losing business without her services. He is useful to me and I promised I would make the suggestion to you.'

Tony paused at the door. 'I don't figure I owe Saadi anything. Hell, no.'

Hasman lifted both hands from his desk, palms up. 'It is not a matter in which I would normally interfere. You may take as many of the women as you wish, but this one cannot be important to you, a cheap little dancer from a club.'

'I'll send her back,' said Tony. 'What with one thing and another, I don't get to see her all that much. She's a smart kid – dancing isn't the only thing she can do.'

Hasman smiled dryly as he dismissed him. The subject was of no interest to Hasman. Women were chattels, unreliable and un-predictable. Child-bearers, nothing more.

Tony went back to his quarters and gave orders for a truck to be ready for him at first light, with a driver. He had less than three hours to pass. He thought about having Elvira sent in to him since she was to go back to her master – the almighty nerve of that Saadi, squatting up there and taking pictures of him and passing them on to old man Hasman. Putting the black on Tony Dimarco, the creep! He promised himself he would lean hard on Saadi the next time they met.

He decided to catch some sleep alone. If things had worked out right, he might have been giving the old business to Louise Vannier instead. Soon, maybe.

He was getting a strong impression that his days in Ahminad might be numbered. Too many complications settling in. Abu Hafidh, for instance. The way he was beginning to operate, he could snarl it up.

Tony lay back on his bed, arms folded behind his head and staring at the ceiling, figuring the angles to himself. He could wait maybe a week or so, until he knew for sure that ten thousand bucks were lodged in his account. He had Richard Ahmin dangling. Maybe Richard Ahmin would still be there when Tony decided it was time to be moving on.

It had been an easy number so far. Nice pickings all round. The real trick was not to hang on too long. In Casablanca he might put out a few feelers, meet some guys with ideas. It was a big country, a hell of a big country. Plenty of room for an operator who had what it took, and this time Tony would have the advantage of a handy balance in the bank. He wouldn't have to scratch about. No sir.

Elvira came in without knocking. She dropped her wrap and stood by his bed, drowsy with sleep, her full lips petulant, and naked as a jay.

'Beat it, baby,' said Tony. 'I gotta get some sleep. I don't have the time.'

'I think you are one dirty pig of a man,' said Elvira. 'Where you been all night? You got another woman? You tell me that? You look at me and tell me that, hey?'

'You go back in the morning,' said Tony. 'That bastard Saadi can't manage without you, you hear that? We're all washed up, baby.'

Scowling, Elvira got in beside him in a very determined fashion, kneeling and looking down at him, holding a breast in each hand like a trader offering a pair of lemons for sale.

'I seen them,' said Tony. 'They're okay, you're okay all round, kid. Now I'm tired, so be a good kid and take off.'

She slid down beside him. She lay very still for a few moments. Shining and aromatic hills and valleys, warm and breathing beside him.

If he heaved her off the bed there would surely be a fight, and he didn't feel right for that. He closed his eyes and pretended he was going to sleep and it didn't fool either of them.

'You one tired old feller,' she whispered softly. 'You send me away you make me nice present first.' Her cunning hands started their job on him, knowing fingers moving over him delicately and surely. 'You liking that, hey?'

'Hell,' murmured Tony. 'You're a little bitch.'

Elvira laughed, her mouth hard against his neck, her hair spreading over his face, coaxing him to the inevitable conclusion. He had little time left then for sleeping.

TEN

To exercise authority successfully over a mixed group of colleagues, some of whom know themselves to be at least as talented as the boss, demands a degree of skill not given to all bosses. The problem of leadership, when the party is far from home and when local difficulties have multiplied all of a sudden, calls for very special qualities if morale is not to slacken.

In view of what had recently been happening in Ahminad, and particularly because of the three casualties they had suffered, Lepelov had tightened things up so as to keep a closer control over what his colleagues were doing. Adopting the role of a martinet, he had issued a number of directives which were to apply to everyone, regardless of status.

They were to keep out of the town, unless on a specified mission that had been approved by himself, and then only with adequate safeguards – most of all at night. There were to be no more casualties, that was official.

All those wishing to leave the domestic compound were to sign themselves out in a register and obtain a temporary pass from Oleg, the Security Officer, giving relevant details to cover their absence. They were to conduct themselves as inhabitants of an armed camp in unfriendly territory. That also was official.

Except for those away on essential duties, all meals were to be taken together. Obligatory parades under the supervision of Lepelov himself. Meal times to be strictly observed. And so forth. This was not a hotel.

Lepelov addressed the assembled company, including the domestic staff they had brought with them, at an early breakfast in the large dining-room. They all knew what had taken place in the town during the night, that surprise attack on the armoury and the fire.

'We must be on our guard at all times,' he said. 'We all have important duties to perform, and the regulations I have issued are to be obeyed at all times. Is that understood?'

There was a grave nodding of heads all round the room. The senior members of the party had long suspected that Lepelov was not up to the job, but they had their own careers to consider – and three colleagues had already died.

'Any breaches of discipline will have serious consequences for the offender, no matter how essential to our mission he may consider himself,' said Lepelov. 'We have no room here for those who cannot accept discipline. We face a difficult situation here, but we will conduct ourselves as goodwill ambassadors of our country, and we will act accordingly. Have you any questions?'

There were none. They were under orders, and Lepelov could make or break any one of them.

'The meal will continue,' Lepelov announced, and sat down at the top table.

The Russian delegation had been accommodated in a large villa that had been originally designed as a private hotel. As a commercial venture it had never enjoyed more than a moderate success since it was in the wrong part of the town to attract the better visitors, so Hasman had requisitioned it for the Russians. There were plenty of bedrooms, some tennis courts long out of use, and an area of over-grown garden with some fountains that had not sprinkled for a long time.

The dining-room faced a side road, a handsome room with three tall windows which were wide open at this early hour.

Breakfast was proceeding in a suitably subdued manner, and those who harboured any mutinous thoughts about Lepelov's bureaucratic prohibitions kept their thoughts to themselves. They would grumble later, when Lepelov was not within hearing. The old boy was obviously scared that he was losing his grip: three casualties and so far no sign of any retribution being demanded. That would not go down well at the Kremlin.

The three small metal canisters came sailing in through the open window, one each. They bounced against the opposite wall and fell to the carpet. One rolled under a table, and all three of them immediately began to squirt their blinding pale vapour.

For a moment there was no reaction because nobody there had been thinking of the possibility of an attack through their very own dining-room windows in the bright morning sunlight.

Then the panic broke and there was a concerted rush for the only door, with no effete nonsense about women being first, because the vapour had risen and spread with alarming speed in that crowded room and there was a lot of furniture in the way. Tables and chairs were being tossed around, and crockery shattered underfoot.

From his end of the room Lepelov shouted orders to which nobody there was paying any attention at all, and he was waving his napkin about which only spread the choking gas still wider. A female secretary of ample proportions who also doubled as a code and cipher expert had got herself jammed in the doorway, and as she felt the press of bodies shoving at her behind she had a fit of screaming hysterics, which effectively rendered her quite immobile and beyond advice.

A large mining engineer, his eyes streaming, more or less walked over her to liberate himself, and he was not the only one. There was plenty of muffled coughing and cursing and blind colliding amid the broken furniture.

One grenade would have been enough to clear the room in short order. Three of them together made it a scene of complete chaos temporarily.

One young man, more agile and enterprising than the others, reached one of the open windows with his handkerchief over his mouth. He managed the ten foot drop to the outside road, and if his sight had been less affected he would have got a glimpse of one of the assailants rounding the corner.

Yusuf had been delighted when Abu chose him as one of the party for this lightning raid. Mossou had had his fun the night before, and Yusuf regretted that the grenades held only tear gas stuff and not high explosives – that would have been good. All the same, he had liked hearing all the noise in there, the screaming and coughing and choking, women as well – that made it extra exciting. He wished he could have been in there to see it all.

He saw that one come down from the window and lean against the wall, wiping his face. Yusuf made a rude finger sign and took off round the corner.

The other two were waiting for him, scowling at him for hanging around when the job had been done. Abu had given them strict instructions, and he had counted them out one grenade each, no more; he had given them just the one target that morning.

The way Yusuf saw it, Abu was too cautious. If they had been given more to throw they could have done some real work, in the *souk* or on any of the crowded streets. That would have made people remember them. They could have jammed the traffic, rolling grenades out into the busy streets, watching the panic all around.

Yusuf now saw himself as a seasoned man of action, and said so. The other two, older men and less adventurous, told him to shut his mouth and obey orders if he wished to remain one of Abu Hafidh's men. Throwing a small canister through an open window did not make a man a hero. Any boy could have done as well. There had been no danger.

Before they split up Yusuf was warned to be at the meeting place on time or he would have to make his way back on foot because the jeep would not wait.

Yusuf swaggered off to inspect first of all the damage that had been done to the Army place in the night. He should have been there last night, with old Burabin and Abu. That had been a fighting man's job. The next time they had something like that planned Abu couldn't leave him out. He was as good a man as any of them.

What a pity Abu had searched them before they left. Nothing to throw. Not a gun or even a knife to work with.

There were soldiers on guard by the blackened ruins of the armoury. Peasants with guns trying to act like real soldiers. They ought to be ashamed to show themselves to the people after last night.

Yusuf lounged against a nearby wall, grinning as he smoked a cigarette. They thought he was just another spectator. They didn't know what he really was, which made him feel good.

He made some very disparaging comments about sons of cross-eyed she-camels who carried guns and pretended they were fighting men, and they were unable even to protect their own property. They were warriors, were they? Then Allah preserve the country! Encouraged by the sniggers of some of the bystanders, his comments became bolder and more explicit and highly insulting.

Inured to public abuse, their morale understandably at a low ebb, the troops ignored him, which provoked Yusuf to further excesses.

It was gratifying to be thus the centre of attraction for a space, although Abu had given them stringent orders about avoiding public places: Abu was over-fond of giving orders, Yusuf concluded.

The amusement palled when a Sergeant with the build of a bad-tempered gorilla shoved his way to the front and offered to ram Yusuf in the privates with the end of his gun if he didn't move off sharp.

So, unloading some parting insults which included reflections on the Sergeant's antecedents, Yusuf took himself out of the danger zone. He sat at an open-air café and listened to the talk while he drank his mint tea. All manner of wild and exciting rumours were circulating, and not only about the business at the armoury in the night.

Something disastrous had happened at the place where those Russian foreigners lived. Nobody yet was quite certain what, but it had surely caused a lot of panic; there had been an ambulance and a doctor there, so it must have been serious.

Yusuf had to resist the temptation to enlighten them. They would never know that the polite young man sitting there in their midst was himself one of that intrepid team – a dedicated patriot who knew no fear.

Nobody appeared worried or sad that the Russians had met with some kind of a catastrophe. Let them go back where they came from. Ahminad could manage without them and their progress, whatever that might be. People were saying that the curfew was coming back, and it was believed that the foreigner Dimarco was taking the army over and this would mean that life would be more difficult than ever. It was agreed that Colonel Marhaba was a useless old fool, but at least they knew what to expect from him, and he was one of their own, a native born gentleman, not a barbarous stranger who treated them like dirt.

There were too many foreigners. They had brought all the troubles with them. That was clear to any sensible citizen. Greybeards wagged, portending yet more disasters to come. There was much discreet whispering about Abu Hafidh, and Yusuf would have dearly loved to inform the company that he was one of Abu's trusted lieutenants, a picked man who scorned danger. One of the heroic band they were whispering about.

More immediately, he was wondering where he could find himself a woman at that early hour. He had no money to pay for one of the women in one of the houses. It would be an affront to his virility to have to pay for it now, and the morning's activity had sharpened his appetite considerably.

Before he left that morning, Abu again

had seen fit to forbid him to involve himself with a woman, with the excuse that he might talk indiscreetly in bed, and the fewer people who knew he was in the town the safer he would be. But then Abu was not a well-endowed young man who had not been with a woman since that Russian on the hillside days ago, and that was far too long for any healthy man. A woman would round off the day that had begun so well.

It would be no good hanging around the whores quarter. It was too early and he knew he would never find one ready to give it away free, the dirty bitches. He hung around the market for a while, watching the women doing their shopping, but they were all too busy to bother with his approaches, they had men of their own, and some of them told him roundly what he could do with himself. There was no demand for Yusuf's services. They could not know what they were missing.

He needed a widow young enough to be still wanting a man, or a married woman whose husband worked far away from home. He found neither.

Long before the appointed time he was squatting in the shade by the broken walls of the abandoned *fondouk* outside the town.

Nothing to smoke. A disappointing end. Next time Abu sent him out he would make sure it was for a night operation. There would be more scope then for a man of his ability.

The other two arrived, one by one and from different directions. They had nothing to say to him and invited nothing from him. He was still a boy, a novice. They had completed a simple mission on time. So what was there to talk about?

Mossou appeared with the jeep. He had slapped some grey paint on it to cover the Russian identification marks. He pulled up in a swirl of dust, and called out cheerfully, 'all is well with you?'

'*Fissa,* quick, little one,' said the leader as they got aboard. 'We are victorious. Could we be anything else?'

Mossou said it was good and drove them off very quickly, demonstrating his skill at finding the firmer ground where their wheels would grip and his unerring judgement where it seemed there was no room for the jeep to pass between the outcrops of broken rock. It was a whirlwind ride under the afternoon sun.

Tony Dimarco had been detained at Casablanca longer than he had intended. He had collected the gas masks, and he had posted that important air-mail letter. Then in a water-front bar by the *Bassin Delande* he had run across an old associate from the Katanga days, the Portuguese Silvao. There was a strong whisper that something of interest was being arranged for the near future.

Not being a man of substance himself, or with any following, Silvao had no precise details – but it might be just right for Tony. An investment in a quick one-off operation. Tony had declared himself interested because Silvao had his ear to the ground – he would be happy with a very small percentage of the take if and when it happened.

Tony had promised to look after him in due course, on the principle of nothing for nothing. Okay? They had worked through a succession of drinks to demonstrate mutual trust and goodwill, while Tony waited for Silvao to drop the name he needed, the name of the guy running the business, after which he wouldn't need Silvao.

It took time and Tony was paying for the liquor at this stage. Silvao was no mug and his belly was lined with zinc.

Pierre Loumay was the guy. He had arrived in Casablanca yesterday, and Silvao thought he knew where they could find him. They would find him together. Where Tony went Silvao went and would not be shaken off.

They toured the hotel bars and the dives. Loumay had been seen here there and everywhere else. Last night. Silvao sweated through a series of monosyllabic phone calls with Tony at his elbow looking more and more uncompromising and skeptical. Pierre Loumay was no longer in Casablanca, or if he was nobody was ready to say where.

Clearly Silvao did not have enough pull, and Tony told him so without bothering to wrap it up. Chalk it up, boy. The next time it might come through. Tony picked up his truck and driver and set off back to Ahminad, many hours later than expected.

Of Lepelov's team of experts very few had escaped undamaged. The hysterical female who had been trodden on in the rush to the door was in hospital and unlikely to be much use for some time, and a replacement would have to be brought in forthwith if the cypher traffic was to be handled promptly. A middle-aged communications engineer, subject to asthma, had not found an intake of CS gas any good for his chest, and would also certainly have to be returned.

Red of eye and shaken, most of the others were in a poor state, including Lepelov himself who had been furthest from the one and only door when the grenades exploded, and who had thus been one of the very last to get clear of the room.

When the power of speech had been eventually restored to him, Lepelov had been on the telephone to Hasman with his immediate demands: an armed guard on the premises night and day, and protective shutters to be fixed on all outside windows, plus a personal assurance from Hasman Abdullah Ahmin that he was taking every step to apprehend the offenders, and Hasman naturally gave him such an undertaking, with expressions of much regret at the outrage.

Later, when he felt more fit for battle, Lepelov called on Hasman and invited him to consider the reaction that might be expected from Moscow when Lepelov's report reached them.

'It will surely shake official confidence in our position here, Excellency,' Lepelov announced gravely. 'I may well be required to present you with what may appear as an ultimatum. It is clear the situation here is rapidly becoming untenable, I may be instructed to ask your co-operation – I refer to the introduction of our own security guards forthwith. We have already discussed this.'

'We have,' said Hasman flatly. 'It does not appeal to me.'

'It would of course be only a temporary expedient. It is also not possible for the present conditions to continue. We are agreed on that?'

'We are,' said Hasman.

'Good,' said Lepelov briskly. 'So we must be protected, Excellency, in the best way possible in the circumstances. Because of the irresponsible actions of some dissidents we find ourselves in a position of some danger. Since you are unable to guarantee our safety, it will surely be reasonable to permit us to defend ourselves. Yes?'

Hasman pursed his lips. He had enough imagination to see where this was leading. Fifty or a hundred Russians, with their own officers and their own weapons – it would be easier to open the door to them than to get rid of them. And where would that leave Hasman Abdullah Ahmin?

Lepelov's profile was as sharp as his tone was incisive. He said, 'we have men who would deal effectively with this Abu Hafidh of whom we are hearing too much. Already three of my people have been murdered, one of them a defenceless young woman, and I have yet to hear that any arrests have been made. Now there has been this savage attack this morning, indiscriminate and unprovoked. Excellency, I am asking how long must we tolerate this lawless state? Moscow will expect a speedy and satisfactory answer. Is that unreasonable?'

Lepelov was leaning lightly on the desk, his tall, spare figure dominating the room. There was much more that he had to say.

The phone rang, and Hasman was happy at the interruption because the scene was shifting too far from his control.

Colonel Dimarco had returned. He was waiting outside. The Colonel was to come in. The Colonel was never more welcome.

As he replaced the phone, Hasman smiled and said, 'Colonel Dimarco arrives most opportunely. He has now taken command of my armed forces. Matters will be handled differently now, you will see.'

Tony came in, greeted His Excellency with respect and nodded at Lepelov.

'Hi,' he said cheerfully. 'I hear you fellers ran into some grief this morning. Too bad. I picked up a load of gas masks – might even spare you one or two. How's that?'

'Excellency,' said Lepelov with dignity, 'we will continue this discussion at a more convenient time.'

'Don't let me break it up,' said Tony. 'I can wait.'

Lepelov bowed politely at Hasman and took himself off.

'He should break both legs,' Tony remarked. 'I got the gear, all my boys on the Richard Ahmin detail have already been issued with a mask. If Abu tries anything he'll come unzipped. Maybe tonight.'

'Tonight,' repeated Hasman gently.

'We can't hope to stop him sneaking into town,' said Tony. 'It's wide open, not like in the old days with the wall all around, but he won't be leaving with Richard Ahmin, I guarantee that.'

'The alternative we considered.' Hasman cocked his head slightly to one side as though trying to remember. 'A foolish attempt at escape, with tragic results ... yes?'

'I just been briefing Prystocki,' said Tony. 'He knows the score, he'll be okay.'

'If it should happen,' said Hasman, 'I

would like it to be as public as possible so that I am not connected with it.'

'I can arrange neutral witnesses. Do it in the street outside, if we have to. We can charge my guys with being too trigger-happy afterwards. That suit you?'

'It would,' said Hasman.

'That clears you,' said Tony. 'What about the girl? Louise Vannier? Do we let her go?'

'I will order a formal investigation into Richard Ahmin's death,' said Hasman. 'That will take time. She will wish to be present. You keep her until then.'

'Check,' said Tony. That solved a problem. If Louise Vannier got out of Ahminad too soon, before that ten thousand dollar credit came through, she would surely have it cancelled – that would be a high price to pay for a corpse.

If she needed a shoulder to cry on, Tony would be available and he'd be ready to take it on from there. Grief made plenty of women sexy. It was a well-known fact. So Tony might score with her after all. With a bonus of ten thousand bucks.

ELEVEN

Lieutenant Prystocki had brought him a mixed bundle of newspapers and magazines. Few of them were less than a week old, but at least they would help to pass the time.

'A very kind thought,' said Richard Ahmin blandly.

'Like to keep you happy, sport,' said Prystocki. 'Orders from the top. You are a hot property.'

'My thanks to Colonel Dimarco, or is it General Dimarco now? I hear old Marhaba has dropped out.'

'You hear too much,' said Prystocki.

'And the Russian delegation,' said Richard Ahmin. 'That must have been most entertaining.'

Prystocki gave him an odd look. 'Have your fun,' he said, and went out.

Richard Ahmin was leafing idly through a copy of *Paris Match* when the picture slid to the carpet. He picked it up and sat looking at it for a long time. It was not a good picture, but the faces were clear enough. His immediate reaction was one of amusement at such a clumsy attempt, and he understood why Prystocki had looked at him so strangely. Dimarco and Louise together in some night spot. So he was to assume the worst.

How little any of them knew Louise. Tony Dimarco, the brash bandit who put a cash value on anything he did, to imagine Louise might ever let herself be interested in trash like Dimarco.

He tore the picture up and dropped the pieces in the wastepaper basket. Now that the house had been made into an armed camp he was allowed out into the garden – there were always sentries about. At night he could hear them clumping around on the roof.

Aziz had been doing some cleaning up; he had his wheelbarrow loaded with refuse, and he was leaning pensively on a rake when Richard sauntered past. There had been no word from Abu for some days. Abu had been busy.

Without stopping, Richard Ahmin murmured, 'Be sure you are at home tonight, old one.'

Aziz scratched about in the dry soil. Of

course he would be at home. Where else? Richard Ahmin passed on to inspect the display of flowers his mother had planted and tended with such care and pride in the old days: the lush purple and violet bougainvilleas, the flame-coloured hibiscus, the roses that had been her special care, the scarlet geraniums that stood hot in the sun always.

His mind was full of Louise. He was not going to permit her to put herself at risk any longer.

In the evening Prystocki visited him. That had become normal practice. Richard would offer him a drink, and it would become a social occasion. Two men drinking whisky and talking, almost like friends. Not prisoner and guard.

But there was a difference this time. Prystocki was in uniform, but had no holster. This was the first evening he had arrived unarmed. Not a subtle young man, he was clearly expecting to notice some change in Richard Ahmin because he had noted the torn scraps of that picture in the wastepaper basket.

Richard Ahmin poured the whisky. 'Happy days,' he said.

When Prystocki lowered his glass he found himself looking at the little gun that had appeared in Richard's hand. They were both standing.

'You crazy?' said Prystocki.

'It's little but very lethal at close quarters,' said Richard. 'You have a car outside?'

'In the road. Listen, sport, you'll never make it–'

'–With you beside me I will. We are leaving together, Lieutenant, and we'll be so close and snug that if they shoot me they'll shoot you. If you do anything I don't like, if you shout to the men on the roof, or give any kind of warning, then I will have to kill you.'

Prystocki shook his head. This wasn't the way it was supposed to be. They had marksmen on the roof, and the spotlight. They'd be expecting Richard Ahmin on his own sometime in the evening. The gates were unlocked. They were to let him get as far as the road, they were then to let him have it, with the spotlight on him.

'You don't have the nerve to pull this off.' Very carefully Prystocki put his empty glass down, and wiped his hands together.

'We'll give it a try,' said Richard Ahmin politely. 'If it fails you will be dead and so will I.'

'For God's sake!' said Prystocki. The guy meant it, he surely did. He was serious. He had that look on his face. Crazy like a fox.

Richard had linked his left hand under Prystocki's right arm, keeping them close together. The gun in his right hand was hidden in the fold of his jacket, inches from Prystocki's body.

'I couldn't possibly miss, could I?' said Richard, as they began to advance to the door. 'When we get outside, Lieutenant, be sure you don't look behind you, just keep walking with me. Say some prayers if you wish, they might be appropriate.'

The garden was in darkness as they came out to the short drive down to the gate, and there was the heavy scent of flowers.

Prystocki whispered something, and Richard Ahmin could feel the heat of his body and tightened his hold. They had taken a few steps down the drive when the spotlight came on, stabbed about and caught them, throwing their joint shadows before them. They walked on, stiffly, awkwardly, but together.

Richard Ahmin felt the skin on his back crinkle as he waited for the crash, the bullet that would kill him even before he heard it, and Prystocki's breathing was loud and uneven. Richard pulled him closer so that they might have been a pair of drunks helping each other home, not too steadily.

Up on the roof the two marksmen exchanged looks. There must have been some switch and nobody had thought fit to pass it on. Goddam officers. So let the Loot-enant handle it his way.

They reached the open gates. Prystocki wiped his streaming face, and the tension was going from his body. Now they were moving out of the spotlight. There were some men in the road, the witnesses to the unfortunate demise of Richard Ahmin.

There was also Prystocki's car, an Opel, left-hand drive, parked by the wall. Locked.

'The key,' whispered Richard Ahmin. 'Quickly.'

Prystocki found his nerve. There just might be a chance now. 'In my pocket,' he said. 'You'll have to let me go... I can't get at it like this.'

Richard Ahmin stepped quickly back and brought his gun out to cover Prystocki's belly. The edge of the spotlight still held them, one of the sharpshooters on the roof saw enough of what was happening, he couldn't get a clear sight of Richard Ahmin, but he got off two rapid shots that chipped the wall over their heads and not too far away.

Prystocki ducked automatically and Richard went down with him, clubbed his gun, and hit Prystocki smartly on the nape of the neck to help him on. Now the angle of the wall hid them for a while. There was shouting up at the house, and the spotlight was jittering about, unable to reach them.

Foraging in Prystocki's pockets, Richard found the key ring. The planted spectators on the other side of the road had begun to move forward inquisitively because the wrong man was on the ground. Richard shot over their heads. Once was enough, and they dispersed at speed into the darkness.

He got himself into the car. Now he had to drive past those open gates, through the light streaming from the roof. He sat as low as he could and let the car surge forward.

Those men on the roof knew their business. They hit the car twice during the split second they had it in their sights. If Richard had been sitting upright the first shot would have blown most of his face away, and the following shot splintered both rear windows. Then he was beyond the gates and into the shelter of the wall, able to sit up and drive properly and with his headlights on.

Dimarco and Hasman would be hearing about this within a few minutes. He didn't think there was another Opel in the town, so he wasn't going to spend much time driving around. The only public telephone was in the main post office and that would be shut now, it was also in the wrong part of the town for his purpose.

He left the car in an alley on one of the less respectable districts. If it wasn't found before morning it would be minus its wheels and other movable parts.

Cautiously he made his way on foot across the town, just as he had done with Abu when they were boys together setting out on some forbidden excursion into the native quarter. Nothing had changed much with the years, and the smell was the same – Ahminad had always been short of drains in the older parts.

Aziz had his modest dwelling on the ground floor of a large building that was mostly derelict, almost impossible for a stranger to find on his own. By the light of a smokey oil lamp that flickered alarmingly in the gloom, Aziz let him in without a word, turned and led him across a cavern of a room that smelt of dried herbs and old fruit and the mustiness of aged brickwork. It had once served as a warehouse, for vegetables and fruit.

Aziz inhabited a room at the back, for which he surely paid no rent. There was a courtyard where the smell of camels and mules still lingered over the worn cobbles. As a boy Richard Ahmin had found the place highly exciting.

Aziz had little furniture. There was a bed in one corner, a wooden table, two chairs, a mat, and a charcoal stove for cooking. A widower for many years, Aziz lived the simple life of a solitary old man. Richard's mother had tried in vain to get him to move into better accommodation. Nobody was quite sure how old he was, but nobody could remember the gardens at the villa without Aziz there to attend to them.

He placed the lamp on the table, spread both hands open to show that all he had was at his guest's disposal, and waited.

'I have to get word to Miss Louise at the hotel,' said Richard Ahmin. 'She must know I am here–'

'*Barak allahou fik* – God bless you,' said Aziz. 'You are free of the house, it is not fitting for a man to be made a prisoner in his own house. This will make the lady happy.'

'Can you get to her quickly?' said Richard.

'*Inch-Allah,* if God wills,' said Aziz. 'They will be looking for you, master, so I will be quick.'

'*Salem aleikoum,* peace be with you, old one,' said Richard Ahmin. 'Tell her I am safe.'

Aziz shuffled out. He could move with speed when he chose, a bent old figure of a man, conveniently hard of hearing when necessary, regarding nobody, and noticed by nobody.

Richard Ahmin sat down to wait. This was one of the first places Abu would call at when he visited the town at night. For emergencies there was a rear exit that entailed some tricky wall climbing and a choice of roofs to be negotiated at no small hazard. Richard could remember trying that route once as a boy, with Abu, for a lark. He wondered if he could still manage it.

It would take a troop of good soldiers to seal the area off effectively. How soon would the news reach Dimarco? Prystocki had said that Dimarco was out of town, picking up a load of gas masks down in Casablanca. Tony Dimarco didn't miss a trick. Prystocki invited him to figure to himself what was going to happen to Abu and his boys when they arrived one dark night to toss the gas bombs around. Instant liquidation for sure.

So Richard had surmised that the air-mail letter was now in transit. Which brought some loose ends into his mind.

For instance, didn't Dimarco know about the clumsy picture? Prystocki had known. But had it been his own idea? Was that why Prystocki had come unarmed? To coax Richard into doing just what he had done?

That walk out had been easy. Too easy? But then they hadn't known he had the little gun. What a pity there had been no time to ask some pertinent questions before he had got so involved with Prystocki.

He calculated that he had now been at liberty about fifteen minutes. If Tony Dimarco happened to be still out of town, that was on his side, because Dimarco was the only one who could get things organized properly.

Tony Dimarco thought so as well. When Prystocki arrived in a shaken condition to report how he had been taken for a sucker so shamefully and by a gentlemanly amateur at that, Tony wasted little time taking the hide off his unlucky Lieutenant. That would come later.

Every available man was sent out on

armed patrol, some even on foot. They were to scour the town and find that Opel. Promotion and a cash bonus to the guy who put a slug in Richard Ahmin.

'Anybody answers you back,' snapped Colonel Dimarco as he dispatched the posse, 'pull the bastards in. It's time we cleaned this place up ... but get that guy.'

Hasman Abdullah Ahmin was going to jump around when he heard the news. So Tony decided to duck that one for the time being.

Taking Prystocki with him, he drove like the clappers across town to the hotel. That would be Richard Ahmin's most likely objective.

'Where in hell did he get hold of a gun?' said Tony. 'You're supposed to have searched the place. Kee-rist, boy, can't you do anything properly? How come you missed the hardware?'

Prystocki shrugged and sucked his teeth and said nothing. What could he say?

When they reached the hotel Tony sent Prystocki round to cover the rear because it was unlikely that Richard Ahmin would enter by the front door or leave by the front door.

'You let him con you again,' said Tony,

'and you better take off for the hills because sure as hell I'll take you apart.'

They were both armed, and Prystocki already had his revolver out as he trotted round to the domestic side. He didn't think Richard Ahmin would be at the hotel. He would be too smart for that. He was a cool bastard.

In the vestibule Tony Dimarco discovered that Miss Louise Vannier was dining, in the dining-room, and at the sight of him striding over to her in martial fashion in full uniform, she put down her coffee cup and if she was happy to see him she concealed it very well.

His face was heavy and dark, and his jaw jutted in the old Mussolini manner. Without removing his cap, he dragged a chair up, planted both fists on the table.

'Okay, baby,' he said softly. 'Where is he?'

Louise moistened her lips. This wasn't last night's would-be seducer.

'Good evening, Colonel,' she said. 'Where is who?'

'Richard Ahmin,' he said. 'He got out.'

She smiled. 'That's good news. You mean he has escaped?'

'You didn't know?' He glared at her. 'Don't fool with me, baby, I'm not in the mood.'

213

'I know absolutely nothing about it,' she said. 'Would I be sitting here if I did, Colonel? I think it's marvellous. How did he do it?'

Tony got to his feet. 'Upstairs,' he said, reached across and pulled her up and held her arm tightly.

'You needn't do that,' she said coolly. 'I'm coming.'

He walked her out of the dining-room. The manager and a few of the residents watched and nobody interfered. He took her up to her sitting-room and made her sit well away from the door. Then he placed himself wherever he could cover the door, and he had his revolver in his lap.

'Like old times,' he said. 'You and me here.'

'You're a fool,' said Louise. 'He won't come here.'

'If he wants you,' said Tony, 'he'll have to come. And if he don't want you, baby, that's okay with me.'

'What about our arrangement?' she said.

Tony smiled at her. 'He's a dead duck. I can still collect. What's to stop me? You? You won't be going any place.'

'I see,' she said evenly.

'I bet you do. I got it all sewed up tight.'

'We should have expected as much,' she said, 'dealing with a rogue like you. I don't think there's a single honest instinct in you. You're ready to cheat everybody.'

'You're breaking my heart,' said Tony. 'Now suppose you tell me where he got that gun? Did you pass it to him? But you only saw him once–'

'That's right,' said Louse. 'I gather he used it successfully. He didn't want to take it, but I'm glad I made him.'

'Goddam,' said Tony softly. 'You are a conniving little bitch – and I was doing you favour.'

'Coming from you,' she said, 'that's quite a testimonial, Colonel. So Richard fooled you after all. You know, he won't come here, he's much too clever for that, he'll know you're here.'

Tony undid his tunic and spread his legs more comfortably.

'Looks like we'll be spending the night here, you and me. You're the bait, baby – so when he shows up I'll blow a hole in his belly. Then you and me, we'll make some sweet music together. How does that grab you?'

She stared at the carpet, her mouth suddenly dry, praying that Richard would

215

stay away because Dimarco would certainly do what he said.

There was a knock on the door. Tony covered it with his revolver in silence. She opened her mouth to shout a warning, but she was too late. The door opened, and it wasn't Richard outside.

TWELVE

Lieutenant Prystocki came in, pushing a bent old figure in front of him in a tattered striped *djellaba* with the hood up.

'Look what I got,' said Prystocki. He pulled the hood back. With his skinny neck and narrow old brown face, Aziz was like a tortoise emerging from its shell.

'I picked him up hanging around the back,' said Prystocki. 'I thought I knew the old goat. He works in Richard Ahmin's garden, boss.'

'Does he now?' said Tony Dimarco. 'What's his story? What's he doing here at this time of the night? Hey you, old man – what are you after?'

Aziz joined the tips of his fingers together and bowed slightly, his wrinkled face quite blank.

'He acts deaf,' said Prystocki. 'But I reckon he hears good enough.'

'You leave him alone,' said Louise. 'He's only a harmless old man.'

Prystocki shook the old man backwards

and forwards, almost heaving him off his feet. It was easy.

'Where's your master, old man? You seen him tonight? Is that why you're here? Talk, you old buzzard.'

'He comes to see me sometimes,' said Louise. 'There's nothing wrong in that – leave him alone.'

'Nobody downstairs ever saw him before,' said Prystocki. 'That's what they tell me. When he saw me he tried to beat it, so I brought him in. I figure he knows something. I've had ideas about him for some time. Like me to lean on him a little?'

'Next door,' said Tony. 'Listen, old man, you gonna be sensible or do we have to push you around? You hear me?'

Aziz shifted his head from one to the other, in polite interest, saying nothing.

'No!' Louise began to get out of her chair. 'Don't you touch him – he can't know anything!'

Tony Dimarco shoved her back and slapped her face just hard enough to hurt.

'We'll let the old boy talk for himself,' he said.

'He'll talk,' said Prystocki. He shoved the old man into the bedroom and kicked the door shut behind him. Louise folded her hands tightly in her lap and tried desperately not to listen. Aziz was too old to stand any rough treatment, and she was sure he had come to the hotel to tell her something – about Richard? That was more than likely. Richard had always been fond of the old gardener.

Tony Dimarco watched her speculatively. They could hear the rumble of Prystocki's voice in the bedroom. Then a silence and Louise closed her eyes. No sound for several minutes. A horrible interval that had to be listened to and there was nothing to hear, yet.

'Please,' she pleaded, 'this is too inhuman … he's such an old man – how can he possibly help you?'

'He works for Richard Ahmin,' said Tony, 'and he comes sneaking around the back where he's got no business to be.'

Prystocki's voice sounded again, louder and more emphatic, not coaxing now.

Abruptly Louise jumped to her feet and ran across to the bedroom door. She wasn't quite fast enough. Tony Dimarco was after her, grabbing her by the hair and swinging her away so that she fell on the carpet, and he was looking so angry that she thought he was going to kick her.

He stood over her, swinging the revolver in one hand, frowning, his lower lip out-thrust.

'Of all the crazy bitches,' he said. 'What the hell do you think you can do in there?'

The bedroom door opened and Prystocki came out. 'He passed out, never said a goddam word. Got a hide like leather. I burned him a little. Didn't do any good.'

'Watch her,' said Tony.

He went into the bedroom. On the rumpled bed where he was planning soon to give the full business to Louise Vannier he looked at the old man's untidy body, and swore softly. There was the smell of scorched flesh.

Prystocki had stripped the old man, and he had been using a cigarette end where it should have been most effective. Hell, the old man should have been screaming. His skinny hairless chest pumped up and down fast. You'd think he'd been running up a mountain.

Tony Dimarco filled a glass with cold water in the bathroom and tossed it in the old man's face. It didn't make any difference. He didn't even try to swallow. Just lay there and panted like crazy. Quick and noisy.

In the other room he found Louise sitting with her face in her hands. Prystocki had lit a cigarette, this time he was smoking it.

'Tough old bird,' he said.

'They always talk in the end,' said Tony savagely.

'Not at his age,' said Prystocki. 'He's liable to kick it. Hell, he's nearly there.'

'Bring him round and try some more,' said Tony. 'Use your knife and let him see some blood – and don't let him pass out before he talks.'

'You'll kill him,' said Louise tonelessly. 'Don't you understand that he's an old man and he doesn't know anything? You've frightened him and he's all confused ... how can you possibly expect him to talk to you?'

'Okay, so you try,' said Dimarco. 'You're so smart, maybe he'll talk to you.'

The phone rang. It was the manager, agitated and nervous. One of Hasman's staff was telephoning urgently. His Excellency wanted the Colonel immediately at the Residence.

'Tell him I'm coming,' said Tony sourly. He put the phone down and swore picturesquely. He had been expecting a scream from Hasman, but this was sooner than he wanted.

The other two waited while he stood and glared out of the window and it was clear

Colonel Dimarco had things on his mind and wished for no untimely interruption.

He was remembering that he had left his car out in the front, and that hadn't been smart for a start. While it was there Richard Ahmin wouldn't come near the hotel. Yet the hotel where his girl was must be his objective. He wouldn't dump her. That picture had set him going. Everything would have worked nicely if it hadn't been for that gun – and that slob Prystocki.

Tony was still betting on the kind of man he thought Richard Ahmin was, and he didn't think he was going to miss.

He swung round and glared at Louise in a sudden surge of lust. By God she had it all and he was going to get her before the night was over.

In recent weeks Richard Ahmin had got used to his own company. There had been no choice, and at the back of his mind there had been an enduring belief that he wouldn't be a prisoner too long. It would have been very different if he had been confined in a prison cell, he was honest enough with himself to know that.

He sat on a wooden chair and watched the yellow flame of the oil lamp throwing its shadows on the walls, and the room was so dim and quiet and remote that he could well understand that it might be right for old Aziz who needed nobody when his day's work was done.

Richard remained untroubled until over an hour had passed and Aziz had not returned. Then he began to suspect that all might not have gone well with the old man. He was a sharp old boy, and he had his wits about him, he also knew the town backwards. But he should have been back by now.

There were two cigarettes left in his case, and Richard smoked them without tasting anything but dried grass. He began to prowl about the tiny room, trying not to look at his watch too often, and failing.

Without a sound the door opened, and Abu Hafidh stood and smiled at him. Abu wore a suit, dark grey and slightly old fashioned, the jacket buttoned high; it was his old business suit from the days when he had been his own master in his own shop.

'God is good,' he said. 'I see you well, old friend?'

'Very well, Abu.'

'We heard in the town that you had made

223

fools of them,' said Abu happily. 'So they are running about and looking for you. I knew you would be here. Where is the old one?'

'He went to the hotel to tell Louise,' said Richard. 'He's been gone over an hour, Abu. I'm worried.'

We were near the hotel,' said Abu. 'Dimarco's car was there. I do not like that.'

'I dislike it very much, Abu.' Richard was making for the door.

Abu stood in his way. 'That would be foolish,' he said quietly. 'They are looking for you. If they find you it will all be for nothing and to no purpose. Is that good, Richard?'

'I'm not leaving her there with Dimarco.'

'If they take you will that save her?' said Abu. 'I have men with me. If she comes to any harm it will be because we are all dead men – and I do not intend to die just yet, if God wills.'

He lifted a hand and left as silently as he had entered, and reluctantly Richard Ahmin had to resign himself once more to the inglorious role of passive spectator. Abu had been right of course – it would have been nonsense to risk being picked up on the street. If Dimarco's car was outside the hotel that meant Aziz had run into more than he could handle. Dimarco must have moved fast.

Tony Dimarco rang his own headquarters. There was only the night duty man there. Everybody was out on patrol, as ordered by the Colonel. No information yet. There had been urgent calls for the Colonel from the Residence. Tony said he would take care of them and banged the phone down.

'Now listen good,' he said to Prystocki. 'Hasman's got his bowels in an uproar, so I gotta go and hold his hand. I'm taking the old guy with me. Stick some clothes on him fast. You stay here with her, okay? If I can pick up a coupla spare men I'll send them to you. But you watch that door, and if Richard Ahmin shows before I get back you let him have it. Clear?'

Prystocki agreed it was very clear. Richard Ahmin wouldn't make a monkey out of him a second time by God.

'He better not,' said Tony. 'It'll be your head, buddie.'

Then he rang down and gave the manager explicit instructions: the vestibule and the front of the hotel had to be cleared right away, no exceptions, and that went for the manager himself as well.

'I want nobody around down there,' Tony snapped. 'You got that? Two minutes from now.'

The manager declared himself more than happy to oblige. There would be no audience to whatever the Colonel had in mind.

With the senseless body of the old man slung easily over his shoulder like a bundle of rags with bare, brown feet dangling, Tony Dimarco made his way down the stairs and across the empty vestibule and out to his car.

He was going to present the old buzzard to Hasman as evidence that they had been doing something. They would bring the old guy round and squeeze him a bit and he would talk, and if he kicked it then – what the hell. He knew something about Richard Ahmin. He would talk.

The car was parked by the ornamental bushes. The tree-lined avenue was empty. He glanced up at the front of the hotel and there were no inquisitive faces watching.

He dumped his load in the back seat, slid his revolver back into its holster. As he straightened he felt the hard and sudden pressure in the small of his back, and he knew too well what it was.

So he was ready to heed the quiet voice

226

behind him as it said, 'Careful, Colonel. It would please me to kill you now. Put both hands on top of the car and do not turn.'

He did what he had to do. He had done this business himself before, but not on the receiving end. He felt his revolver being slipped out of its holster, and he gazed longingly up at all those empty windows where there was nobody to see what was happening to him below. Hijacked on his own territory, by God. The sole Commander of the armed forces in Ahminad.

Now there were two guns at his back, and at least two men. They must have been hiding in those goddam bushes.

'If you have killed the old one,' said Abu Hafidh, 'you have little time to live yourself. Where is the lady?'

'Up there. You'll never get her – you don't think I'd leave her without an armed guard. I got six good guys up there. You try it.'

'Get in the car and drive where I tell you,' said Abu.

When they moved off, Abu was beside Tony Dimarco, sitting sideways so that he kept both guns on the Colonel's belly and out of sight from the road. Burabin crouched in the back with the head of the old Aziz in the crook of his arm, whispering

227

over the unconscious old man – fierce whispers of a blood-thirsty nature directed at the back of Dimarco's neck.

Abu was giving clear and rapid instructions: *turn here and here, and now down here, and into that alley, Colonel, and under that old arch … there will be enough room …* invariably there was, just enough.

At an intersection where there was some light, they came on a pair of Dimarco's men who recognized the car and its driver and gave their Colonel a couple of casual salutes which were not acknowledged, the miserable bastard.

Tony Dimarco was concerned with matters more important than military etiquette. He knew who sat beside him, and he had no reason to believe that Abu Hafidh would hesitate to use those guns. So he went on doing precisely what he was told, and he was steering the car into a part of the old town that he didn't know.

He made just one comment. 'You guys'll never pull it off,' he said. 'You got it all loaded against you.'

Abu smiled. 'We have an old proverb which says that the camel does not see his hump. If you had been wiser you would have left Ahminad before this. After tonight you will not be needed, certainly not by Hasman Abdullah Ahmin.'

'Big talk,' said Tony Dimarco. 'I'll have to see you back it up before I start crying. You had a lucky break, that's all.'

'We have you,' said Abu very politely. 'Turn down here slowly and stop by the wall. My fingers are itching to shoot you.'

THIRTEEN

Richard Ahmin heard them coming in this time – footsteps and Abu's quiet voice advising somebody to be very careful. He had the door open when Abu appeared, shoving Tony Dimarco in front of him, and there was no gladness on Dimarco's face as he was pushed out of the way in a corner so that Burabin could carry the old man across to his bed.

'Sit,' said Abu.

Tony Dimarco sat on the floor with his empty hands in front of him and his legs spread, not a dignified posture for a Colonel in full uniform. He gazed with interest around the dim little room that was now so crowded.

Burabin had been examining Aziz's lean, brown body, and he had seen the burn marks. Without a word he turned and crossed the room and kicked Dimarco twice very quickly, once in the stomach and then in the face.

Stooping over Dimarco and speaking very

evenly, Burabin said, 'If the old one dies, I am giving you my promise that death will come for you so slowly that you will be weeping with welcome for it. You hear me, son of a syphilitic she-camel?'

With his hands folded over his bruised mouth, Tony Dimarco was in no state to reply, but his eyes were eloquent.

Abu quietly coaxed Burabin away. 'Aziz still lives,' he said, 'he will not easily die, I think. Go now and tell Mossou to bring Doctor Moulay and say to him that I have sent for him and quickly.'

With a lingering glance at Dimarco that was full of malevolence, Burabin went out. Tony Dimarco wiped his mouth. Some teeth had been loosened, and there was a sharp ache in his belly.

He was in a spot where the rules didn't apply, and his mind was busy fashioning some bargaining point – there had to be one.

'What about Louise?' said Richard. 'What did you find out about her?'

'We were too late,' said Abu. 'She is still in the hotel, she is well guarded, he says – we caught him as he was leaving, with Aziz.'

Richard turned his attention to Dimarco, and there was more menace in his pale blue eyes than Burabin had conveyed with his promise of a lingering death.

'Well, Dimarco?'

Tony Dimarco found himself able to speak. 'She's okay. Prystocki's looking after her, in her room.'

'He said he had six men guarding her,' said Abu. 'I did not believe he could spare that many to guard one woman in her own room.'

'Only Prystocki,' said Tony. 'The rest of the guys are out on patrol.'

'And where were you taking Aziz?' Richard asked.

'He wouldn't talk. Hasman was shouting for me, I was going to take the old guy with me.' Tony Dimarco's voice became more confident. 'You ready to listen to a proposition?'

'From you?' said Richard Ahmin with utter contempt. 'I listened once before, Dimarco, and I found the proposition had a very bad smell. Fortunately I had a gun when I needed it.'

Tony Dimarco grinned painfully. 'That goddam little gun. Okay, but listen – your only safe way of getting out of here would be in my car with me driving. That make any sense to you?'

'So you're switching sides again,' said

Richard. 'What makes you think anybody would trust you now?'

'I'll be right there with you,' said Tony. 'I phone the hotel first and tell Prystocki, he brings the lady down, and we beat it fast. I got the only car in the place that won't be stopped on the road, not with me driving. Think about it, but don't take too long because Hasman don't like the way things are working out.'

Burabin had drifted back. He stood listening, with a brooding expression on his face, mostly directed down at Tony Dimarco. He said Mossou was bringing the Doctor quickly.

Abu pointed at Burabin. 'Look well at this man, Dimarco,' he said. 'He shot the headlights off your truck up in the hills. He will be at the front of the hotel when the lady is brought out. If there is anything that does not please him he will shoot you first, and Burabin never misses.'

Burabin nodded, the professional accepting his just tribute. 'Then I shoot the guard. The lady will be safe. I shoot that one first. Correct?'

Tony Dimarco wiped his mouth again. This was business talk if ever he heard it. Burabin squatted down on his hunkers and gazed into Tony's face as though learning it by heart, and it was not an experience that Tony Dimarco enjoyed.

'You will be alone in the car,' said Richard Ahmin, 'so there will be no reason for Prystocki to be suspicious, I will be there when you phone him and I will tell you what you will say. If there is the slightest hitch you are a dead man. From where he will be waiting Burabin could shoot the buttons off your tunic without tearing the cloth.'

Tony Dimarco gazed up at the three of them. 'I'm the only guy risking anything.'

'Your idea,' said Richard Ahmin. 'It's up to you to make it sound right with Prystocki. If you can't do that, we'll forget it here and now and find another way.'

'Such as?' said Tony.

'It won't concern you,' said Richard. 'You won't be leaving here. There are cellars down below where you can relax while we do some arranging, and if Aziz dies we will bury you down there.'

'I believe you would,' said Tony Dimarco. 'You're one hell of a gentleman.'

'I try to be,' said Richard Ahmin. 'It's my English blood.'

Mossou came in with Doctor Moulay, a slight little man in a shabby dark suit who greeted only Abu Hafidh and went over to the bed with his bag. He expressed no surprise when he saw the nature of his patient's injuries, he had seen too much of man's inhumanities to man. Opening his bag he busied himself in silence while they waited, and Burabin was staring fixedly at Tony Dimarco, a hawk watching its intended prey.

Finally Doctor Moulay pronounced his patient in no immediate danger. He would survive. Tony Dimarco began to breathe again.

Mossou volunteered to stay with the old man and carry out the Doctor's instructions. Richard Ahmin took some notes from his wallet and offered them to the Doctor who nodded without looking at them. It would have made no difference to him if there had been no money. Mossou escorted him out.

'On your feet, Dimarco,' said Richard, 'and listen very carefully while I tell you how we are going to do this.'

Tony Dimarco got up and listened very intently since his own neck was going to be on the block.

Lieutenant Prystocki was helping himself

liberally to Louise Vannier's whisky. He needed it because she had made it abundantly clear what she thought of him for what he had done to old Aziz, after which she had ignored him as a very low form of life indeed. Anybody would think the old guy mattered to her. Women had crazy ideas.

There was a phone call from HQ – Prystocki's Opel had been found. No hubcaps, no radio aerial, no spare wheel, no petrol. Otherwise okay. And no Richard Ahmin, naturally. Prystocki whispered very profanely and took more of the free whisky. The night ticked along.

The manager rang. Please could his establishment return to normal? Guests had been confined to their rooms as the Colonel had ordered, and now they were complaining. So what was he to tell them?

'Tell them to go to bed,' said Prystocki. 'Hell, it's close on midnight. Tell them you're all closed up for the night. Colonel Dimarco's orders. And you can stay by the phone, bud, and put my calls through.'

The manager yammered a little, until Prystocki invited him to take it up in person with the Colonel when he returned.

Then came a call from the Residence.

Hasman himself, wanting to know where the Colonel was, and Hasman sounded distinctly displeased. He had summoned Dimarco half an hour ago, where was he?

Prystocki said the Colonel was on his way, with an important prisoner – no, not Richard Ahmin, not yet. The Colonel must have stopped off somewhere on the way. His Excellency was assured that everything was under control.

The conversation ended abruptly while Prystocki was still talking, and he had a tinge of uneasiness when he remembered that he had been the one in charge of Richard Ahmin's guard, so Hasman wouldn't be pinning any medals on him.

Now where the hell was old Tony boy? Maybe the old guy had kicked it on the way and Tony was having to dump him somewhere. Could be.

When one of his staff informed him that all the armed guards had been withdrawn from their area without notice, Lepelov immediately tried to phone a strong protest to Hasman, but found His Excellency quite elusive because he had more pressing matters to attend to.

In view of what had gone before, Lepelov

found the situation unsatisfactory, and the general attitude of Hasman's underlings little less than insulting.

Evidently the time had come to present an ultimatum to Hasman: he must either now agree to allow the representatives of the Soviet to protect themselves adequately on the lines previously discussed, or Lepelov must consider himself free to refer the matter back to his government with a view to a possible withdrawal. Then there would be a heavy claim for compensation to Russian personnel, including three deaths. And Soviet property – an expensively equipped jeep, for instance.

Then the news was brought to Lepelov: Richard Ahmin had broken out of custody and had not been recaptured, which explained why Hasman was unavailable.

Now was the time to bring pressure to bear on Hasman. For so long Lepelov had been urging him to transfer Richard Ahmin to a proper prison, and now Lepelov had been proved right, of course. He had all the ammunition he would need to bring Hasman under firm control, this very night.

The reports going back to those powerful ones in the Kremlin would take on a more healthy tone, and the career of Lepelov would surely look brighter.

Without going through the formality of asking for an audience because he knew full well that he would be put off again, he changed into his most sober suit and issued strict orders that nobody else was to venture outside. He, alone, was going to see Hasman Abdullah Ahmin.

When the senior members of his little staff ventured to remind him that there might be some danger, Lepelov gave them a stiff and dignified reply as befitted the representative of a Great Power in an obscure foreign town – who would dare to touch him? In a car flying the official flag of the Soviet Union? It was unthinkable.

He drove carefully out of the gates where there should have been armed men on duty. He glanced right before turning out into the road under the trees.

From the shelter of a buttress in the wall some yards away to the left, Yusuf darted forward and tossed a gas grenade in through the open window. It hit against the windscreen and rolled under the seat out of reach, and instantly began to work.

Instinctively Lepelov put his foot down before he realized what had happened, and

239

the heavy car surged forward momentarily out of control, with Lepelov leaning frantically back from the wheel as the fumes began to envelop him from below.

His vision already gone, Lepelov tugged at the wheel, the car ran against a tree trunk, jamming the door on the driver's side, and by the time he could crawl across the two seats and fight his way out by the passenger's door – no small matter since he could see nothing – he was in a very sad state indeed: coughing and retching, his lungs red hot and raw, and his eyes so blinded that he had no notion where to crawl, and he took his scalding breath with him wherever he turned. Eventually he just collapsed on the ground, and rubbed his face on the road in agony.

Yusuf waited long enough to satisfy himself that he had not been hanging around the gates to no purpose, and then took off smartly into the shadows by the wall.

He had talked Abu into allowing him a roving commission just for the night in the town – one canister, and a stern warning that he was to bring it back if he couldn't find an effective target. What better target than the chief Russian pig himself? Beautiful work by Yusuf, and all by himself.

When Lieutenant Prystocki heard Tony Dimarco's voice on the phone, he said, 'God's sake, boss, where you been?'

'Shut up and listen,' said Tony. 'There's been a switch – four minutes from now I'll be outside the hotel in the car, and I want you to bring her down – you got that?'

'Sure.' A switch, the man said. 'You been cooking up something, Colonel? Clue me in – old Hasman's been shouting for you like crazy all night–'

'Shut up!' said Tony. 'Bring her down to the front of the hotel and don't ask so many goddam stupid questions!'

End of message.

Prystocki grinned. Tony sounded edgy, so he was up to something, and somebody was liable to get scorched real bad, and it wasn't going to be Lieutenant Prystocki. No, sir.

He poured himself the last of Louise Vannier's whisky. She hadn't said a word to him for fifteen minutes. One frosty dame.

'We're going downstairs,' he said. 'You and me. The Colonel's taking over.'

She looked at him with no favour. 'Where are we going?'

'Search me. He didn't say. You better ask him.'

241

'Suppose I refuse to move?'

'You're nuts.' He poured the neat whisky down his throat.

'I'll scream,' she said. 'I'll rouse the hotel.'

He looked her over from head to foot. 'Then I'd have to shut you up and carry you down. You feel you gotta make a noise, that's okay with me, baby, it won't get you no-where. The boss wants you down below in a coupla minutes – we'll do it any way you like.'

She walked out of the room and down the empty stairs, with Prystocki's hand firmly under her arm. The manager peered dis-creetly from his office door, but offered nothing. He was happy to see Prystocki off his premises without any gunplay.

The whisky had got to Prystocki. He was holding Louise more tightly than needed, and his step was just a little too deliberate and heavy.

When they came out into the open air there was no car there, just the tree-lined avenue and the bushes. Louise tried to free her arm. Prystocki was leaning on her, grin-ning at her, backing her up against a pillar by the door, his face a few inches from hers.

He shifted his grip. His arm came low

down around her waist, ramming her against him, just for the hell of it. Tony had given it to her, and he had one eye on the road for Tony's car. No harm in copping a quick feel.

She kicked him hard on the shin and brought her knee up sharply in unladylike fashion so that he had to release her and bend over, hissing with pain. The dirty bitch.

Louise began to run, away from him, and down along by the bushes, and too late she realized it would have been more sensible to get back into the hotel and up to her room, because he would soon catch her in the open once he had got over the damage.

Burabin was squatting in a clump of oleanders, about fifty yards across from the front of the hotel. He had his rifle across his knees – he was too good a marksman to risk having sweaty hands on the trigger before he had to go into action. He saw them come out, and he also waited for the Colonel's vehicle to arrive.

He did not like what he then saw happening on the steps. A man should not handle a woman so. Any woman.

He saw her beginning to run uncertainly, looking round. He saw the other leaning at the pillar and reaching for his gun. That was enough.

Burabin's rifle had a silencer. For shooting inside the town it would be foolish to make too much noise. He needed just one shot. *Phut.*

Prystocki slid down beside the pillar, an expression of mild surprise on his face and a small, dark hole just above the bridge of his nose.

Bewildered, Louise had halted at the sight of Burabin emerging from the bushes, with a gun. She didn't know him, but he had to be on their side. At least he had shot Prystocki. He was beckoning her over, with what was no doubt an encouraging smile on his face. It seemed pointless to go on running – where to? Apparently Dimarco was meant to be coming for her.

And there were the lights of a car now coming fast down the avenue. So she ran across and Burabin parted the bushes and showed her where to hide without having to say anything.

In his black Mercedes Tony Dimarco swept up to the front of the hotel and braked hard, and knew that it had gone wrong when he saw Prystocki's body sprawled on the step – and no girl.

Instinct told him to get the hell out of it. Casimir Prystocki had been fast with a gun, and he lay there on his back with his revolver half drawn. He had met somebody faster.

Tony Dimarco felt the sweat starting behind his ears and in the small of his back as he glanced across to those goddam bushes. They had warned him he would be covered all the time. That guy with the long, dark face, the one who had been so quick with his feet – he was out there somewhere, waiting and ready to lay him alongside Prystocki.

There was no percentage in this. He needed a truckload of his own guys to come rolling down the avenue. Instead there was that jeep parked in a garden off the end of the avenue, watching to make sure Tony Dimarco didn't try anything fancy on his own.

Like what? They had him blocked off. And where in hell was the girl?

He took a good and careful look all round. He had kept his engine running. So suppose he just took off fast? A calculated risk? He watched Prystocki's body as though waiting for it to get up and do something.

When he decided to get out of the car he

had his revolver ready. Nobody was going to make a duck-shoot out of Tony Dimarco. He caught a glimpse of the hotel manager's face chancing a look out of his window, and on the upper floor windows some curtains shifted a little.

He went up the steps and looked at Prystocki's body. Plumb between the eyes. Fancy shooting. Real good.

Facing vaguely in the direction of those bushes he raised his revolver over his head in acknowledgement, a kind of salute. And the revolver was whipped out of his grasp in the very instant he heard the shot, from down there to his right. The revolver slid over the step behind him and he lifted both hands now over his head.

Burabin emerged, shuffling sideways and fast, with his rifle ready, waist high, and Louise Vannier coming after him.

Tony Dimarco cleared his throat. 'Okay,' he said thickly.

'In,' said Burabin. 'You drive, mister. Lady, you pick up the guns, then you sit in front.'

Tony Dimarco was ushered into the car, with the rifle prodding his kidneys. Louise sat beside him with the two revolvers in her lap. Burabin took them from her and lowered his rifle out of sight. He squatted behind Dimarco, tapped him warningly with one of the revolvers behind his right ear.

'You drive where I tell you, mister. You stop for nobody. Correct?'

'Correct,' said Tony Dimarco.

'Now drive, mister.'

The little party waiting in the jeep had become uneasy at the delay down in the front of the hotel, and they were too far away to see what might be happening. Abu Hafidh was about to investigate on foot when they saw the black Mercedes coming up, Dimarco driving and with Louise beside him – as arranged.

'Thank God for that,' said Richard Ahmin. 'It's working, Abu.'

They were to follow the Mercedes at a discreet interval over the route Abu had indicated, which would also help to ensure that Dimarco behaved.

The Mercedes came abreast of them.

'Look,' said Abu quickly. 'Up there – Hasman's car–'

An old-fashioned Cadillac, yellow with a black top, was turning into the avenue. There were two men in the front and they looked like soldiers. In the back sat Hasman himself, not too much of him visible over the high coachwork.

Tony Dimarco recognized the Cadillac bearing down on them. There wasn't another like it south of the Med. Hasman's Hearse, they called it.

This could be the payoff. Hard against the bone behind his ear he felt that gun.

'Drive,' whispered Burabin.

The Cadillac swerved towards them, flashing its lights. Hasman was leaning forward in his seat so as to get at the window, and when he got there he was waving at Colonel Tony Dimarco to stop.

Tony Dimarco yanked savagely at the wheel to avoid a head-on collision, and there wasn't much room because of the trees. Burabin was at the rear window with his rifle, while the startled soldier in the front of the Cadillac was still scrabbling about to get his gun from down by his feet because Hasman Abdullah Ahmin was shouting at him to stop the Colonel's car.

Just before the Cadillac clipped the rear wing of the Mercedes, Burabin, leaning well out, shot twice in rapid succession – two moving targets coming at an angle and at speed, but so near that Burabin could not miss. Hasman first, and then the worried soldier.

There was a clang and a tearing of metal. The Mercedes rocked, the Cadillac veered sideways and stopped and the driver got out with both hands above his head.

'We stop now,' said Burabin. 'You come.'

Tony Dimarco abandoned the impulse to make a break for it. This was a massacre, so why add to it? He got out and Burabin took him over to the Cadillac, and he needed no prodding with a gun. He had been hired to see Hasman stayed alive, and now old Hasman had a hole in his head.

On Burabin's morose face there was a satisfied expression. For a long time he had been wanting to get Hasman Abdullah Ahmin in his sights. The Number One target that had become so invisible in recent weeks. Burabin felt he had not disgraced himself.

The jeep arrived. Abu Hafidh and Richard Ahmin joined Burabin.

'I didn't want this to happen,' said Richard.

Burabin glanced at him bleakly, snapped his fingers and shrugged.

'We could expect nothing else,' said Abu. 'I did not think Hasman would come out.'

'It is good I shoot him,' said Burabin.

Richard ran over to the Mercedes. Louise

was getting out, and he caught her up in his arms so that her feet were off the ground.'

'Are you all right?' he demanded. 'Are you?'

'Never better,' she said breathlessly.

'Good.' He put her down. There was no time for anything more. They had all heard the truck coming down the avenue. Tony Dimarco's truck with its spotlight lighting up the scene. There would be Dimarco's men in the back.

'No shooting,' said Richard Ahmin quickly. 'We don't have to fight our way out of this. Dimarco, they're your lot, order them back to barracks.'

He ranged himself on one side of Dimarco, and Abu was on the other, and Abu had a gun sticking into Dimarco's kidneys. The light fixed on the three of them in the road. The truck slowed and then stopped when Dimarco lifted his hand.

'Go on, tell them,' said Richard Ahmin quietly. 'Send them back. Hasman's dead – so there's no point in it any more. You're out of a job here...'

'I'll make a deal with you,' said Dimarco.

'No deals,' said Richard. 'Not until they're out of the way.'

'You're a cool sonofabitch.'

From the front of the truck a voice called: 'Hey, Colonel, what gives? Hasman pulled us off the detail – we been looking all over for you–'

'Okay, you guys!' Dimarco shouted. 'Back off and get back to barracks. I'll see you there.'

There was a pause. The truck didn't move. Off to one side Burabin worked the bolt of his rifle. Tony Dimarco suddenly stiffened.

'Git!' he shouted. 'You guys gone deaf? Hasman's dead – you beat it back, you hear?'

The truck reversed slowly, turned and began to move off up the avenue, and the faces of some very puzzled soldiers watched over the tailboard.

'That was nice,' said Richard Ahmin softly. 'We must all hope it stays like that for the rest of the night. We've had all the shooting we need.'

'I figure this makes you the boss around here,' said Tony Dimarco. 'I just gave you some good co-operation. Right? So what's in it for me?'

'You'll be on your way out of here at dawn,' said Richard.

'Just like that?'

'Just like that, Dimarco.'

'We had an arrangement.'

Richard Ahmin smiled pleasantly. 'No ten thousand dollars. You over-reached yourself this time.'

'Bastard,' said Tony Dimarco, but without much feeling.

'The world is wide,' said Richard, 'and I won't need you here.'

Somewhat later that night, Richard Ahmin stood in the room that had been the study of the late Hasman Abdullah Ahmin. Louise and Abu Hafidh watched him expectantly, and he was feeling oddly deflated after the events of the last few crowded hours.

'Excellency,' said Abu quietly, 'there is now much to be done.'

'I don't know if I am the right one to do it, Abu … I don't think I ever thought as far as this.'

'Think now,' said Abu. 'If you leave us we will have nobody, and life in Ahminad will be as bad as before. You do not wish that, Excellency?'

'No,' said Richard Ahmin soberly.

'Your first business will be with the Russians,' said Abu. 'I think they will be ready to leave us now. They are not happy here any longer. I hear Lepelov met with another misfortune tonight. He is not dead, but he swallowed too much of the gas and he is a very sick man now. There was another sad happening tonight outside his house. One of my young men, you understand.'

'Very sad,' Richard Ahmin agreed. 'I hope he will recover.'

'I fear he will,' said Abu.

'Nasty things, gas grenades. We must control these impetuous young men, Abu. We are going to be peaceful and respectable in the future. No more Russians, no more bandits like Dimarco.'

'They will leave when it is light,' said Abu placidly. 'We will search them to see they steal nothing.'

'Dimarco will love that,' said Richard cheerfully. 'Let them have a full tank for the truck, nothing more. Can you raise enough men to see it through?'

'More than enough, Excellency,' said Abu. 'Men like Burabin – there will be no more trouble in the town.'

He bowed himself out. A happy man.

Richard smiled across at Louise. 'I believe the feminine of Sultan is Sultana – how does that grab you, darling?'

She came over, perched on the edge of his

desk, took his face in her hands, and kissed him prettily.

'I'll settle for plain Mrs Richard Ahmin.'

In the grey dawn a solitary truck bumped down the dusty road, heading for Casablanca. The men squatting in the back were not duly perturbed at this sudden reversal in their fortunes, even though they had been very efficiently eased out with nothing but the gear they wore. It had been a sweet set-up while it lasted, and they were confident that old Tony would pick them another.

And Tony Dimarco, reduced in rank but still philosophic in defeat, was already thinking in terms of what might be organized down in Casablanca, by a sharp operator.

As the man said, the world is wide and you never can tell what might be around the corner – another crummy joint like Ahminad. Why not?

This Large Print Book, for people
who cannot read normal print,
is published under the auspices of

THE ULVERSCROFT FOUNDATION